"Thank you for everything you've done," Hunter said.

"It means the world to me to have someone like you in my corner."

RaeLynn smiled at him. "I think often about my childhood, and how different things would have turned out for all of us had we just had some extra support." Her expression changed, and a faraway look filled her face, wistful maybe, perhaps a little sad. He reached forward and brushed her cheek.

"I'm sorry if this brings up painful memories. I wish there was more I could do for you."

The smile she gave him told him that she wanted the same thing, but it wasn't possible. Maybe it was just wishful thinking on his part.

"I hope you know what an amazing woman you are," he said.

"I think the same about you. I never knew a man could be so loyal and faithful and care so deeply for children, especially ones not his own."

He brushed her cheek again, and the look in her eyes brought a deep longing to his heart.

Danica Favorite loves the adventure of living a creative life. She loves to explore the depths of human nature and follow people on the journey to happily-ever-after. Though the journey is often bumpy, those bumps refine imperfect characters as they live the life God created them for. Oops, that just spoiled the ending of Danica's stories. Then again, getting there is all the fun. Find her at danicafavorite.com.

Books by Danica Favorite

Love Inspired

Double R Legacy

The Cowboy's Sacrifice
His True Purpose
A True Cowboy
Her Hidden Legacy

Three Sisters Ranch

Her Cowboy Inheritance
The Cowboy's Faith
His Christmas Redemption

Love Inspired Historical

The Nanny's Little Matchmakers
For the Sake of the Children
An Unlikely Mother
Mistletoe Mommy
Honor-Bound Lawman

Visit the Author Profile page
at Harlequin.com for more titles.

Her Hidden Legacy

Danica Favorite

LOVE INSPIRED

INSPIRATIONAL ROMANCE

LOVE INSPIRED®
INSPIRATIONAL ROMANCE

Recycling programs
for this product may
not exist in your area.

ISBN-13: 978-1-335-40938-6

Her Hidden Legacy

Copyright © 2021 by Danica Favorite

This edition published by arrangement with Harlequin Books S.A.

For questions and comments about the quality of this book, please contact us
at CustomerService@Harlequin.com.

Love Inspired
22 Adelaide St. West, 40th Floor
Toronto, Ontario M5H 4E3, Canada
www.Harlequin.com

Printed in U.S.A.

A new commandment I give unto you,
That ye love one another; as I have loved you,
that ye also love one another. By this shall
all men know that ye are my disciples,
if ye have love one to another.
—*John* 13:34–35

To my husband, who has given me so much support during a rough season of life and who gave me the tools I needed to follow my dreams. I could not have written this book without you.

Chapter One

The foyer in the main lodge at the Double R Ranch looked warm and inviting, but as RaeLynn McCoy looked around the room, all she felt was a sense of foreboding. Why had she come here? She knew better. Had spent her whole life hearing about how she should never set foot in this place. RaeLynn had a personal connection to this ranch, one that she'd promised to never reveal. She was the long-lost granddaughter of Ricky Ruiz, the owner of the Double R. She'd never had any intention of meeting him, but here she was, looking for someone to check her in and wondering if it was too late to turn back. At least none of them knew who she was.

If it weren't for the fact that RaeLynn had a job to do, she'd turn around and walk away. No, she wouldn't have even come to begin with. But the magazine she worked for, *Mountain Lifestyles*, had assigned her to do a story on the Double R Ranch, highlighting its contributions not only to the Colorado ranching community but also to the nearby town of Columbine Springs, which had recently suffered a devastating fire. Without the caring spirit of the Double R, the town wouldn't have made it.

Listen to me. Already writing the marketing copy. But RaeLynn knew better than anyone else about the dark side to the Double R Ranch and its owner, Ricky Ruiz.

Not that that was the story she was

after. No, she would write a feel-good piece that would wow Gerald Stein, the publisher, enough that rather than selling off to the conglomerate that was trying to buy their small magazine, he would let her take over and run it. A corporation would ruin the magazine and its small-town feel.

Mountain Lifestyles served many Colorado communities, and more than that, the people who worked there were a family. They took care of each other, and their readers counted on them for good stories and uplifting news. She'd seen what the company that wanted to buy the magazine had turned other local publications into. Glorified ad circulars that cared more about making money than serving the people of the community. So if saving *Mountain Lifestyles* meant sucking it up and going to the one place she'd promised never to visit, RaeLynn would do it.

She'd banged the bell on the front desk multiple times. With such glowing reviews, you'd think the ranch would have someone staffing the lobby.

RaeLynn turned toward the hallway where the sign said Office, but as she did so, a small child came barreling past her, nearly knocking her over.

"Hey! Be careful," she said.

The little girl stopped and stared at her. RaeLynn had probably spoken a bit too harshly to the kid, but she hadn't expected to be run over.

"I'm sorry I yelled at you," RaeLynn said. "But you do need to be more careful."

"You gotta hide me," the girl said.

RaeLynn looked around. As far as she could tell, they were the only people in the building.

"From what?"

"He's gonna kill me," the child said. She couldn't be more than about four years old, and RaeLynn couldn't see anyone wanting to kill the tyke. It wasn't like that child had literally lived in fear. RaeLynn knew the look of fear. Had lived that life. And she was glad that these children didn't actually know what it meant to be that kind of scared.

"Please," the little girl said. "He's gonna kill me."

The child darted around and then opened the closet door. "Don't tell no one you saw me."

RaeLynn sighed. She'd barely set foot in the place, and already someone was trying to pull her into some kind of drama, and drama was something she was trying to escape in her life. It was almost like God Himself was saying *Here, let Me give you a big fat plate of everything you hate in the world.*

That wasn't fair. She knew God didn't take that level of interest in people's lives. She also knew He wasn't sick and twisted and wouldn't torment someone like that.

A boy who looked to be a few years older than the little girl came running into the room. "Where did she go?"

This must be who the girl was afraid of. Likely a sibling. None of this was her concern. What was her concern was getting checked in so she could go to her cabin and collect her thoughts.

RaeLynn smiled at the boy. "If you're talking about the lady at the front desk, I have no idea. Do you know any grown-ups who could check me in?"

There. She was saving the little girl, but she also wasn't lying. She still didn't know exactly what was going on, and she'd prefer not to.

"Sadie didn't come to work today, and Hunter said that if she did it again, he'd fire her, so we're all pretending like she's here." The boy slapped his hand over his mouth. "You won't tell him, will you?"

Given that she was a paying guest waiting to be helped because this woman hadn't shown up for work, Rae-Lynn would say there was probably a pretty good reason to fire this Sadie, especially since it sounded like this was a common thing.

"I do need someone to check me in. I've been driving a long time, and I just want to get settled in my cabin."

The boy looked thoughtful for a moment. "I was supposed to tell my mom if I saw anybody come up the driveway. But Lynzee let my pet snake out of its cage, and now it's gonna get eaten by a hawk or some other wild animal. My mom said I could only keep it if it didn't get out. So even if I find it, my mom is going to make me get rid of it. Which means I'm going to kill Lynzee."

"That seems a bit extreme, don't you

think?" RaeLynn asked. "She's just a little girl. Surely you don't want her to die?"

He let out a long, dramatic sigh. "No. I'm not really going to kill her."

She smiled at the him. "What's your name?"

"Sam Bennett." A wide grin split the little boy's face.

Great. She knew exactly who he was. And while she knew she'd inevitably have to interview his parents as part of her article, she'd hoped to get her bearings before dealing with them. Not every member of the Double R family had a happy ending to their story.

Ricky's son, Cinco, had died tragically in a bull-riding accident nearly thirty years ago. Because Ricky and Cinco were estranged, Ricky never got to meet the grandchild Cinco's wife had been carrying. Wanting to right the wrongs of his past, Ricky had gone in search of the grandchild. In his search, he'd found three other children Cinco had fathered as part of his extramarital affairs—Rachel, Alexander and William.

But Ricky hadn't found the child he'd been looking for. And that was because that child, RaeLynn, hadn't wanted to be found.

After everything RaeLynn's mom had been through with Cinco and Ricky, RaeLynn wasn't willing to risk getting hurt by her biological father's family.

As far as anyone here knew, RaeLynn was just a regular reporter with a story to write. And she planned on keeping it that way.

RaeLynn smiled at Sam, hoping to convince him to get his mom. "Well, maybe if you explain to your mom that a little kid who didn't know any better let your snake out, she'll let you still keep it. Maybe, instead of trying to find the girl to hurt her, you should try to find your snake and get it back into its cage before it causes any trouble."

The boy looked thoughtful for a moment. "That's a good idea," he said. "You sound like you'd be a good mom. You got any kids? Especially one that's about my age? I mean, I have my friends, but my best friend, Katie, is on a vacation with her mom and dad, and my other best friend, Ryan, has a new baby at his house, so he can never play. So if you have a kid I could play with, I wouldn't have to play with Lynzee all the time."

RaeLynn tried not to laugh as she shook her head. "Afraid not. I don't have any children, and I don't want any."

The little boy gave her a funny look. "What do you mean you don't want any? Everybody wants children. My poppa says that children are blessings from God."

This little kid was quite the character. She kind of liked him.

RaeLynn shrugged. "I had a lot of brothers and sisters, and I had to practically raise them. I'm done with kids."

She didn't know why she'd just told the boy that, since he probably didn't understand. RaeLynn had helped raise her siblings and helped with their babies when they'd had them. It was a fluke that she'd earned a scholarship to college when no one in her family was pregnant or had a newborn.

No, she wasn't going to let having children stand in the way of her dreams. That meant being here, writing the story and getting back to Denver so she could convince her boss she was worthy of running the magazine.

She smiled at Sam. "Listen, I'm sorry I don't have a kid for you to play with. And I get that you're trying to help this lady not lose her job, but do you think you could find someone to get me checked in so I can go to my cabin?"

Sam shrugged. Then he turned, walked to the door and yelled, "Mom!"

Finally. RaeLynn had to admit the kid was kind of cute and funny. She'd reluctantly agree that she liked her siblings and their children. She'd probably like them more if she hadn't been obliged to raise them. RaeLynn had eventually realized the healthiest thing for her was to step away from them and create her own life.

A woman came into the lodge, looking a bit frazzled. RaeLynn recognized her as being Janie Bennett, Sam's mother. "Sam! You know better than to play in the lodge. You're supposed to be at Ricky's with Lynzee."

Sam looked sheepish. "The baby was taking a nap, and Grace said we had to be quiet. But we were bored, so I asked if we could go outside."

Janie gave him a stern look. "This doesn't look like outside to me. And it's definitely well outside the fence. You know you're supposed to stay inside the fence."

"Yeah, but Lynzee ran out, so I had to come after her."

RaeLynn bit back a grin as she remembered what coming after her had actually looked like.

"You should have gotten a grown-up, or at least told someone where you were going. Grace is worried sick."

Janie looked around. "And where is Lynzee?"

RaeLynn gestured at the closet door. "I believe she's hiding in there. She was afraid someone was going to kill her."

Janie looked at Sam. "We've talked about this. You go on back to the ranch house and let Grace know you and Lynzee are okay."

Janie walked toward the closet. "Lynzee, it's safe to come out now."

She turned to RaeLynn, almost as if it were an afterthought. "I am so sorry. It's usually not this disorganized here."

When Lynzee didn't come out of the closet, Janie opened the door and gave a small chuckle. "Sound asleep. She's just at that stage where she kind of needs a nap but won't take one. It's a weird age to manage. She was dropped off so early this morning that I'm sure she's wiped out."

She picked up the sleeping child, held her in her arms for a moment and then gently laid her on one of the couches. "Like I said, it's usually not like this. So tell me, what brings you to the Double R? We aren't open to guests until next week."

Janie walked behind the registration desk and typed a few things in the computer. Then her face fell. "Oh no. You're from that magazine, aren't you? I am so sorry. We've already made a terrible first impression. I didn't think you were getting here until tonight."

While RaeLynn did think this was a bad way to run a business, there was something about the distress on Janie's face that made her sympathetic. Janie was trying to do the best she could, hoping to impress a reporter, and she thought she'd blown it.

"It's fine," RaeLynn said. "I understand. Sometimes things happen. I recognize you from the background research I did. You run the local community resource center. It sounds like you're doing great things with it."

Hopefully, this would ease Janie's mind. Some people got so nervous around RaeLynn when she was working on a story. It was always best to put them at ease.

Janie grinned widely. "Yes. So many

projects. In fact, that's kind of why I'm trying to cover for the gal who usually works the front desk. She's had so many bad things happen, and this job is supposed to be a fresh start for her."

"It sounds like you really care," RaeLynn said. She understood the helplessness in Janie's voice. After all, that's how she'd felt dealing with some of her family members. Janie was choosing to help people. RaeLynn respected that. After all, she was trying to help people, too. Just in a different way.

"Anyway," Janie said, "she's a good kid. Well, I guess she's not really a kid anymore, but she's had a hard time of it, and I'm just trying to look out for her."

RaeLynn smiled. "Your secret is safe with me. I can understand the situation. I'd love to come down to the community center to see the work you're doing. I want as big a picture of the community as I can get for the article. I understand the Double R does a lot for the community center."

Janie smiled. "I appreciate that. My husband has been great with getting grants and things, but I think it would be really good for our donors to see someone taking note of the work we do and getting some positive press."

"Are you getting negative press?" RaeLynn had done her research in advance and hadn't seen any.

Janie laughed. "On the contrary. We're not getting any, other than a few stories when we initially opened. It's hard for small towns to get much notice in the media. We try, don't get me wrong. But it seems like the rest of the world doesn't care about what happens in a small town or about the kind of work we do here."

That was exactly why RaeLynn had to do this. Why, despite all of her misgivings and vows to stay away, she absolutely had to do her story on the Double R and its impact on Columbine Springs.

A man stomped in the front door. "Janie, have you seen my daughter?" He stopped when he noticed RaeLynn. "I'm sorry. I didn't realize we had guests. No one is due until next week, other than that reporter who's coming tonight."

Janie laughed. "Meet the reporter."

The man took his hat off his head and swiped a hand through his hair. For a cowboy, he wasn't bad looking. In fact, if he hadn't mentioned that *D* word, she might have been tempted to flirt with him. But having a child put a man firmly on her Absolutely Not list.

He set his hat firmly back on his head and strode toward them. "Ma'am, I am so sorry. We've had a busy few days here at the ranch. Please forgive me. Ricky would tan my hide if he knew I wasn't here to personally greet you. I'm Hunter Hawkins, the ranch foreman."

Hunter's grip was warm and firm when he shook her hand. She'd always liked a man with a good handshake.

"RaeLynn McCoy, the reporter." She gave him a smile to hide the flip-flop in her stomach at the mention of Ricky.

Her mother had told her to be wary of Ricky. Apparently, Ricky had treated RaeLynn's father, Cinco, badly and had not been very nice to her mother. It was probably a good thing RaeLynn had never known her father, considering her mother always said he was nothing but a drunk cowboy. RaeLynn's stepfathers had also all been drunk cowboys, with varying levels of abusiveness.

If her mom said to be wary of Ricky, RaeLynn wanted nothing to do with him on a personal level. Hunter's statement about Ricky tanning his hide only made her more determined not to let them know who she was. Clearly,

Ricky's bad temper hadn't changed over the years.

RaeLynn gave Hunter another smile. "Don't worry about not having everything perfect for my arrival. I like that. Anyone can put on a good show. I want the chance to see who everyone is. I want to see your hearts."

The man looked slightly relieved. Then he noticed the little girl sleeping on the couch. "What's Lynzee doing here?"

Janie sighed. "It's a long story. Let's just say that she and Sam were fighting again, so she hid in the closet and fell asleep."

He sighed as well. "Maybe it's too much to ask to have Grace watching her. She's got her baby and your son, and I know Lynzee can be a handful. I keep hoping the day-care center will open back up, but it sounds like Jesse isn't rebuilding after the fire."

Janie smiled at him. "Now, stop that talk. If Grace minded, she would have said so. Things are just extra busy today, and I have a disobedient son who will be dealt with accordingly."

Nodding slowly, Hunter said, "I just don't want to be taking advantage of other people's good hearts. Lynzee is my responsibility, and I don't want anyone feeling like I'm foisting her on them."

It was refreshing to hear someone insisting on taking responsibility for their child, especially a man. None of Rae-Lynn's many stepfathers had ever stuck around for very long when they realized what being a father actually looked like. And her sisters certainly hadn't made the best decisions when it came to men, either.

"What about her mom?" RaeLynn asked.

"She died," Hunter said. "I don't have

any family to speak of, and her family has enough problems of their own." He looked around the room. "Where is Sadie?"

Janie gave him a placating smile. "She wasn't feeling well, so I gave her the day off."

"She's pregnant again, isn't she?"

His face darkened, and he looked like he had other choice words to say but kept them inside.

"If she is, she hasn't told me." Janie sighed again. "But I have my suspicions. And it would do you well to get used to the idea so that when she does tell you, you can at least act happy."

"She's already got three kids she can't take care of. You know I think babies are the greatest blessing from God, but she needs to stop having them and do something good with her life. I thought you were helping her get a grant to go to college or trade school."

"I was," Janie said. "And I still am. Even if she is pregnant again, there's no reason she can't start going to school."

He nodded slowly. "And I suppose you're going to ask me to help her out again."

"Don't think I don't know who leaves those envelopes of cash under their mat."

He gave a small shrug. "Even though my wife died, her sister and her kids are still family. If I don't take care of them, who will?"

The resignation in his voice brought sympathy to RaeLynn's heart. She knew exactly how he felt. Technically, many of her siblings weren't really her siblings, just an assortment of stepkids her mom picked up along the way and a few half siblings. But in their family, they'd never differentiated between half or step. They were just family. And RaeLynn had also found herself sending checks, leaving cash and doing whatever else she could to make sure they were all okay.

But the family drama gave her one more reason she shouldn't get involved with these people. Why she was never going to tell them who she was. Yes, she knew Janie was married to her half brother. And part of her was curious to know what he was like. She'd get to know him for the article, but she wasn't going to let him know who she was. She wasn't going to let her other brother and sister here on the ranch know, either.

The only trouble was the illusion of a happy family didn't last in RaeLynn's knowledge or experience, and she was already too overwhelmed with the family she had to let in any more.

All RaeLynn wanted was to get what she needed to write her story so she could save the magazine. That was her priority. Not getting mixed up with these people.

* * *

Hunter took a few deep breaths to collect his thoughts. This was more stress he didn't need. He didn't like the fact that he had to keep leaving Lynzee with Grace. He hated feeling like he was a burden on everyone here at the Double R. Grace had a new baby and should be focused on that, not on keeping his daughter out of trouble. But as he picked up the sleeping little girl from the couch, he didn't know what other options he had.

Then there was the problem of Sadie skipping out on work. He'd promised to help his late wife's sister, but she didn't seem to want to be helped. Sadie already had child services breathing down her neck. If she were pregnant again, how was she going to handle being a mother to yet another child?

Hunter already had more than enough to deal with in his life. Janie seemed sympathetic to Sadie's problems, but she didn't understand that he was always the one to fix them.

He looked over at Janie. "I know Ricky asked me to do it, but would you mind getting RaeLynn settled in? I need to get Lynzee back to Grace."

Janie held her arms out for Lynzee. "I'm headed back there anyway. You take care of our guest."

Lynzee started slightly as he transferred her into Janie's arms. But then she sighed contentedly.

That was the one thing Hunter knew he was doing right. His little girl never wanted for love. When his dad had died, Hunter's mom had moved to the warmer climates of Arizona, promptly remarrying, and starting a new life there. The folks at the Double R were the closest to a family Hunter had. And lately, he felt like he'd been letting them down.

Ricky had given him one job. Told him

his top priority was to make RaeLynn McCoy, this reporter, feel welcome and have the full Double R experience so she would write a good article about the ranch and the surrounding community.

Though people understood the Double R had to cancel reservations after the fire to help the community, now that the community was in the process of re-building, the guests hadn't come back. They'd found other ranches to visit, other places that hadn't let them down.

Ricky always said that a man's word was his bond, and he felt like their rep-utation had been tarnished as a result of the cancellations. In Hunter's mind, it was admirable that Ricky had put taking care of his community ahead of profits. Hunter hoped having this re-porter out here would show not just how good the Double R was but also show the true spirit of Columbine Springs.

He looked over at RaeLynn. "Let me

show you around the place. I apologize for not being here to greet you. We should have been more prepared. But it's fine that you're here now."

To his relief, RaeLynn smiled. "I'll admit, I was a little eager to get here. Please don't worry about any of this. I think it's refreshing that small businesses care about their people and are like a family."

He probably cared a little too much. Everyone knew his threats to fire Sadie weren't serious. "She's my late wife's sister. Felicia might be gone, but the family needs a lot of help. I still feel an obligation to help them."

RaeLynn gave him a sympathetic look. "I understand better than you think," she said. "My family is a little chaotic as well. I do my best to take care of them, but I've also learned that I need to live my own life. It sounds like you need to find a balance."

Hunter laughed. "A balance? That's a good one. I don't know how you do that with kids."

When RaeLynn laughed in response, the comforting sound brought a warmth to his heart he hadn't known he'd been missing. She had a nice smile, a compassionate expression, and although he'd not known her very long, he could tell they were going to be friends.

"That's why I am never having kids," she said.

He stared at her for a minute. "Never? That seems a little harsh."

RaeLynn shrugged. "I spent most of my childhood helping raise my siblings, as well as their children later. I know some people have that maternal longing, but I think I got my fill."

He nodded. "I can understand that. Maybe that's why I always thought I'd have about a dozen of them. I was an only child, and I always hated that it was just me."

Even though he saw where she was coming from, to some extent, Hunter felt a little sorry for RaeLynn. Sure, his wife's family got on his nerves from time to time, but it felt good being part of something bigger than himself. And it felt good knowing Lynzee would grow up surrounded by friends and loved ones who cared about her.

As they started out the door, his phone rang. Usually, he'd ignore an unknown caller when he was with a guest, but with Sadie gone and not answering the ranch phone, it could be something important.

He looked over at RaeLynn. "I'm sorry, give me one second."

Turning, he answered the phone. "Hello?"

"It's Sadie. I'm in jail."

Not what he'd been expecting. As she started to explain, he felt sick. Another drunk-driving arrest. Before she could go into her usual excuses, he cut her off.

"I'm sorry, not bailing you out again this time. I did that the last time, and you promised to get help and quit drinking. Your sister died drinking and driving, and I would think that you of all people could understand that."

He was about to say goodbye when she said, "Wait, please."

"I can't bail you out," he said. "Even if I wanted to, I don't have the money."

"My kids are home with Jennifer. Can you get them?"

Jennifer. The thirteen-year-old neighbor kid who babysat for her when she went out. Meaning all those kids had been left alone all night with Jennifer. Hopefully, Jennifer's parents had probably come by and helped, but he couldn't be sure. Worse, though, was the fact that if social services found out, it could jeopardize Sadie's chances of keeping her kids.

While Hunter firmly believed that Sadie should suffer the consequences of her actions, he also didn't want the kids to suffer. There weren't a lot of foster-care options in their small town, which meant the kids might be sent to parts unknown and potentially separated. These were Lynzee's cousins. Their family. Hunter had to keep them together.

"Did you call Jennifer's mom and dad?"

"I only get one phone call. I called you."

Which meant, once again, it was up to Hunter to fix things. "All right," he said. "Let me see what I can do."

He looked over at RaeLynn. "I'm really sorry. Sadie's in jail, and her kids have been left with a thirteen-year-old. I'm sure everything's fine, because Jennifer's parents are good people, but I need to figure out what to do about the kids. There's already an active social-services investigation going on, and I need to keep the kids safe."

He looked down at his phone. "I'll call Ricky and see who we can get out here to show you around."

RaeLynn reached forward and touched his arm gently. "Why don't I come with you to help? I'm experienced with kids, and I'm sure they're probably scared and confused. Especially if social services are involved."

He should say no. She was a guest, one they wanted to impress. However, the tender but firm look in her eyes told him it would be a waste of time to argue.

"All right," he said. "Let's go."

Chapter Two

As soon as Hunter got out of his truck at Sadie's house, Darla Olson, the baby-sitter's mother, stepped out of her house next door.

"Sadie's done a lot of things in the past, but this one takes the cake."

Hunter nodded. "I know. If it's any consolation, she's in jail over in the next county. I didn't get the call until just now."

Darla nodded. "I was worried it was something like that. I suppose we should be grateful she's not dead."

A car pulled up, and as soon as Eleanor Hopkins got out, Hunter's stomach sank.

He looked over at Darla. "You didn't?"

"I had no choice, and you know it. She didn't come home last night."

"You could have called me," Hunter said, taking a deep breath.

Darla shook her head. "They're her responsibility. It's time she grew up and became a mother to these poor kids."

He didn't disagree. But making sure the kids were taken care of was more important than teaching Sadie some life lessons.

Jennifer stepped out of the house, carrying a wailing baby. "Good," she said. "You can have a turn. Bella hasn't stopped crying all day."

As Hunter reached for the baby, Rae-Lynn said, "I'll take her. You'll have your hands full with the others. And I'm good with babies."

RaeLynn went over to Jennifer, took the screaming baby and cradled her in her arms. The sight touched Hunter deeply. RaeLynn didn't have to come, and she certainly didn't need to step in like this.

Eleanor approached, looking grim. "Sorry I couldn't get here sooner," she said. "It's a big county, and I don't have enough staff. You say Sadie left the kids alone again?"

Again? Hunter ran his hand over his face. Why hadn't Darla looped him in? He looked over at the woman who'd already told him once that Sadie's kids weren't his responsibility. She didn't get it. The kids were still family. Hunter would have dearly loved to grow up with some cousins, and he wasn't going to deny Lynzee that.

"I was just coming to pick them up," Hunter said. "I came as soon as I got the call that Sadie was in jail. She signed some papers a while back giving me rights to help out in case she was incapacitated, and I guess that fits the situation here. I'm going to take the kids back to my house with me."

It was a long shot, and he knew it the second the words came out of his mouth. Especially when the frown didn't leave Eleanor's face.

"I'm not sure that's a good idea," Eleanor said.

"Come on, you know me," Hunter said. "I volunteer at the Sunday school and passed all those background checks. Let them come and stay with me while you look over the paperwork and run your own checks. We both know there's a shortage of foster homes around here."

The look on Eleanor's face told him he'd won. For now.

"Fine. But only because I know how seriously the church takes the background reports they run on the childcare workers," she said. "But you're wrong about not having a place for them. Well, for the baby, at least. I have a family looking to take in a baby."

A baby. "And the others?" he asked.

Eleanor shrugged. "Placing three kids at the same home is nearly impossible."

Hunter knew he had to do whatever it took to keep the kids with him until Sadie was able to take care of them.

"She's right," RaeLynn said, joining them. "That's why I helped so much with my siblings and their kids. It's hard to keep families together."

He glanced over at her, and she shrugged. "Sorry. Didn't mean to intrude. But I've had a lot of experience with this kind of thing."

She turned to look at Eleanor and held out her hand. "I'm RaeLynn McCoy. I realize you don't know me, but I'd like to help if I can."

The sincerity in her voice eased some

of the fear in Hunter's stomach. Having an ally made the situation seem less daunting, especially since Eleanor's expression softened as she shook Rae-Lynn's hand.

"I know you're just trying to make things safe for the kids. I think we can all agree that the best thing for the kids is for them to be together, and they have a responsible family member who loves them. So let's figure out how we can make it work."

Hunter had been hesitant to bring her, but now was glad RaeLynn was here. He went to church with Eleanor and knew she was passionate about helping children, but he wasn't sure he would be able to manage the system and its rules.

"I know your heart is in the right place, Hunter," Eleanor admitted, "but the county has a lot of rules we'd need to follow. I've got a packet I can email you. Give it a read, and I'll come by your place Monday afternoon to go over the next steps."

Hunter nodded slowly. He hadn't expected things to get this complicated. He'd only planned to have the kids until Sadie got out of jail, but it seemed like his life was about to get a whole lot more complicated.

RaeLynn walked with Eleanor to her vehicle, chatting about something as she worked to calm the baby. When Eleanor finally got in her car, Hunter felt himself relax. He hadn't realized how tense he'd gotten, but the slump of his shoulders as she drove away reminded him.

The other two children came wandering out of the house. Little Phoebe, who was the same age as Lynzee, went to him.

"Uncle Hunter."

He took her into his arms, noting that

she was freshly bathed. He kissed the top of her head. "You smell like strawberries."

Phoebe grinned. "Jennifer gave me her special shampoo."

The little boy, Tucker, wasn't talking much yet, but he lifted his arms for Hunter to pick him up, too. Hunter lifted him and breathed in the sweet little-boy scent. He, too, had been freshly bathed.

"Thanks for giving them baths," he said.

Darla shrugged. "They were filthy. I know it's none of my business, but things have been really bad here ever since Sadie's mom left to go take care of her sister in Nebraska."

Hunter blew out a breath. It wasn't anything he didn't know, though he hadn't thought it was this bad. He was just grateful this revelation hadn't come out while Eleanor was there. "Thank you for letting me know. I should have checked in on her more, but it's been so busy at the ranch. We're just coming into the tourist season, and I've needed to get everything ready. But with Sadie in jail, I'm going to have to figure something out. Thank you for taking this on. I know you didn't have to."

He pulled his wallet out of his back pocket and fished out some bills. "I don't know what she promised to pay you, but hopefully this covers it as well as some extra for keeping them overnight."

Jennifer shrugged. "She only promised me twenty bucks. This is way too much."

Twenty bucks to watch all three kids for a few hours was way too little, in his opinion.

"You earned it," he said. "This went well beyond what you were supposed to do, and I'm really grateful. It's nice to know they have some good neighbors who are willing to look out for them."

RaeLynn, who'd been out pacing the yard with the baby, trying to get her to calm down, returned to the porch. "I think her stomach is upset. How has she been taking her bottles? What have her diapers been like?"

Jennifer let out a sigh of relief. "She didn't have very many dirty diapers at all. It's so nice. Tucker's are always so nasty and smelly."

Darla looked thoughtful for a moment. "Now that you mention it, it does seem a little odd. But she has been taking her bottles just fine."

RaeLynn looked over at him. "Do you have the number for their pediatrician?"

Hunter nodded. "Yes, and I'm listed as someone who can make medical decisions."

Early on, the family had agreed it was

best for the kids if another responsible adult could step in if needed. The kids' father had made it clear he wasn't interested, and with their grandmother out of town frequently, it had seemed like a good idea to have Hunter available as an emergency backup.

"Why didn't you guys call me when she didn't show up last night?" Hunter asked.

Darla shrugged. "It was late, and I know how early you get up. I didn't want to bother you. We were scheduled to watch the kids while Sadie worked. But wow, after having them all day yesterday, overnight and then today, I sure am beat. Who knew they'd be so much work?"

Hunter chuckled along with Darla. "I guess I'll find out. Lynzee by herself is a handful, so adding three more will be an adventure."

He glanced over at RaeLynn, who, despite the fussing baby, smiled at him. She sure did have a pretty smile. He didn't know many people who'd smile after being thrown into such an unexpected situation with a screaming baby. Though, he had to admit, since Rae-Lynn had taken her, the baby wasn't screaming, just quietly whimpering.

"I'm going to go over to Sadie's house and get what I need for the kids. Do you have a key, Darla?"

Darla shrugged. "I don't think there is one. She never keeps it locked."

Hunter walked into the house, unable to believe the mess. He didn't think the place had been cleaned since Susan had left, which was saying a lot, considering she'd been gone for at least a month. And this was a house full of toddlers.

"I tried to pick up a little when I was here last night," Jennifer said, trailing behind. "But there's a lot to do."

"Don't worry about it," Hunter said.

"She's not paying you enough to clean and take care of her kids."

"I'm sorry," Darla said, joining them. "Jennifer usually keeps the kids over here. It's too much for me to manage everything I have going on at home, plus Sadie's kids, so I didn't realize how bad it had gotten."

Hunter had been there several times before, but the mess had never been this extensive. He should have done a better job looking out for Sadie. But he had his own life, his own problems. He went into the kids' room, noting that clothes and toys were strewed everywhere, and he couldn't find a single clean thing.

He turned to see RaeLynn, still holding Bella close to her.

"It's probably not worth trying to find anything clean," she said. "Just gather up a bunch of stuff, and we can wash it at your place. I'm assuming you have a washer and dryer?"

He did, but so did Sadie. He'd purposely bought her the set last Christmas because hers had kept breaking down. He'd figured that with three kids, one of the things she needed most was a washer and dryer.

Hunter sighed as he nodded. "Might as well go see what she has in the laundry room. At least everything there will be in hampers."

Phoebe tugged at his pant leg. "What are you doing?" she asked.

He squatted to her level and gave her a smile. "How would you like to come stay with me and Lynzee for a while?"

Phoebe grinned. "Can I bring some of my toys?"

He smiled at her and ruffled her hair. "Of course. Go get your backpack, and put what you want in there."

As he gathered things for the kids, his heart broke at the realization of how bad things had gotten. If Sadie really were pregnant again, she likely wasn't feeling well enough to take care of the kids. It hadn't been a problem with her other pregnancies because her mom had been here. But with this one, Hunter wasn't sure how she was going to do it. And if she were pregnant, he was even more upset to find out she'd been out drinking and driving. What had she been thinking?

He noticed RaeLynn in Sadie's room, gathering things for the baby.

"Is there anything I can help you find?" he asked. "I might not know where everything is, but I might have an idea of what she does have."

RaeLynn gestured around the room. "I think I have all the basics. I noticed car seats in the living room. Have you given thought to where the baby is going to sleep?"

Hunter shrugged. "I'm still trying to figure out how we're all going to fit in my little two-bedroom cabin. It's always been fine for just me and Lynzee, but with everybody else, I'm not so sure. I can probably borrow a couple of the cribs we have for guests at the ranch, put one in my room for Bella. Lynzee has a double, so she can share with Phoebe. We can get another crib for Tucker in Lynzee's room, but it's going to be a tight squeeze."

As he started thinking through all the supplies and things he'd need, Hunter was grateful he had the resources of the ranch at hand. They weren't booked for now, and he was sure Ricky would have no problem letting him use the cribs.

They quickly loaded everything into the truck. Hunter was glad he had one of the bigger vehicles from the ranch. The car seats all fit easily into the back. The baby was still fussing, but once they got on the road, she drifted off to sleep.

In fact, it wasn't five minutes before all three kids were out like a light. He looked over at RaeLynn. "Thank you for coming to do this with me. I don't know how I would've managed alone with Bella screaming like that."

She gave him a gentle smile. "I've had a lot of practice. My sister Andrea's babies all had terrible colic. I think I spent the better part of three years doing nothing but consoling screaming babies. But I do think that Bella is not feeling well, so it might be a good idea to give her doctor a call."

Hunter nodded, but his stomach was in knots. What was he going to do if Bella was sick?

"I will as soon as we get back to the ranch."

He glanced over at her again. "I hope you don't mind my saying so, but you seem awfully young to have raised so many babies."

She shrugged. "My mom didn't make the best choices when it came to men. My dad died before I was even born, and the other guys she met along the way always seemed to come with kids of their own that she ended up raising. I was always expected to help out."

"That doesn't sound like much of a childhood," he said. "I can see why you might not think you want a family of your own."

"I don't think, I know."

The stubborn look she gave him made him wish he hadn't said anything. She'd been good to help him out, and the last thing he wanted was to make her feel like she was being attacked.

"I'm sorry," he said. "I didn't mean anything by it. Just trying to make conversation. Since you took so much time to help me out, we should probably talk about why you're here. Did you have specific questions about the ranch, or should I just give you a brief overview?"

He thought his words would relax her, but it seemed like she was even more tense.

"I don't have my notebook with me," she said. "So if you don't mind repeating yourself later when I don't remember what you shared, I'd love to hear more about the ranch. How did you end up here, and what do you love about it?"

He might not have been able to put RaeLynn at ease, but she'd definitely done that for him. There was nothing he liked talking about more than the ranch. No place he'd rather be. As he talked about how he'd grown up on a neighboring ranch, his father one of Ricky's close friends, Hunter found himself relaxing even more.

Today had not gone as he had expected. And it was going to be a long few days until they had answers about

Sadie. He wasn't foolish enough to think that everything was going to be easy the day she got out of jail, especially now that social services was involved.

It was clear that Sadie had been struggling long before the events of last night. Part of him felt like he'd let her down, that he hadn't done enough to help her. It was the same feeling of helplessness he'd had before his wife, Felicia, had died. She hadn't been happy on the ranch. She'd always had dreams of moving to the city and having a life there. Hunter had always figured it was just a phase. That in time, she'd get over it and realize this was where they belonged.

Sometimes he thought that if he had done a better job of listening to Felicia and finding out what she really wanted out of life, she'd still be alive. A lot of things had been wrong with their marriage, but the biggest had been how much he loved the ranch and, in hindsight, how much she'd hated it. Was that Sadie's problem?

Sadie often talked about getting out of this place, just like Felicia used to. He'd always chalked it up to her needing to grow up and be an adult, but maybe Hunter was the one who'd needed to grow up and realize not everyone loved the ranch like he did.

As they drove on to the ranch, he rolled down the window to breathe in the fresh air and revel in the familiar feeling of coming home.

He'd never been able to get Felicia to understand that feeling, and as he studied the blank expression on RaeLynn's face, he wasn't sure he was passing on just how deeply he loved the ranch to her, either.

Maybe he was, as Felicia used to tell him, just a dumb cowboy who didn't know anything. But there was nowhere else in this world he'd rather be.

The next morning, RaeLynn stepped out onto the deck of her cabin. When they'd gotten all the kids settled, Hunter had tried to take her to the cabin they'd reserved for her, the nicest guest cabin at the ranch. But she'd spied a smaller one, not too far from Hunter's place where she could easily stop by if needed. Though his cabin was slightly set back to give him a little more privacy as the ranch manager, she could still see it from her deck. As she sat sipping her morning cup of coffee, she wondered how Hunter had fared overnight.

A truck pulled to a stop at Hunter's place. RaeLynn recognized the women getting out as Wanda, the ranch housekeeper, and Janie. They retrieved a few containers of what must be food from the back seat. RaeLynn stepped off her porch and started toward them. "Can I help?"

Wanda smiled at her. "You're our guest. You've already done so much. You're supposed to be enjoying yourself, not taking care of everyone else."

RaeLynn had heard that multiple times since she'd arrived at the Double R. Though she knew Hunter was grateful, she could tell he also didn't like having to accept help from a guest. Maybe this wasn't the five-star treatment she'd come here for, but it gave her a whole lot of insight into the character of the people at the ranch and how they ran things. The sense of community was unlike anything she'd ever known. Growing up, no one had helped her family like this. It had just been Rae-Lynn. How her mother had managed when RaeLynn was small she didn't know. But regardless of what happened with their mom, these kids were going to be all right.

"I hate feeling like we're dragging you into all this chaos," Janie said. "It's really not always this bad."

RaeLynn smiled at her. "Please stop apologizing. If it makes you feel better, I grew up in a situation just like these kids'. I wish we'd had a caring community to help us the way you guys are. I know how hard it is when you're dealing with alcoholism." RaeLynn held her hands out for one of the boxes. "Let me take something."

Wanda handed her a casserole dish. "Get this in there before it gets cold. I made an egg casserole for everyone." She went to the back of the truck and pulled out a basket full of fresh laundry.

"That was nice of you to wash all those clothes for Hunter," RaeLynn said.

Wanda shrugged. "We take care of

our own. Plus, that man does not have time to be doing all this laundry."

Janie nodded. "I'm sending a group over to Sadie's house today to clean. We'll make sure everything is in good shape for when she gets home."

RaeLynn nodded slowly. "When will that be?"

Wanda and Janie exchanged glances. "Hard to tell. We've all agreed that the best thing for her is to face the consequences of her actions. No one is going to bail her out. The kids are safe with Hunter. We'll all help Hunter get through it. Sadie's mom needs to stay with her sister, which leaves us to help take care of everything."

The confidence of the older woman's voice brought a lump to RaeLynn's throat. Would her life be any different if she'd had people like these willing to help?

When they got into the house, Hunter

was asleep on the recliner with the baby on his chest. RaeLynn was moved at the sight. Unshaven and clearly exhausted, the man's love for Bella was obvious. It was amazing to think that a man could so tenderly love a baby, particularly one that wasn't his own.

RaeLynn put a finger to her lips, to tell the women to be quiet, but Hunter was already stirring. He stretched and yawned, but his hand remained on the baby, cradling her close to him.

"What time is it? I was supposed to feed the animals this morning."

"Alexander and William took care of that for you," Janie said, setting the laundry basket on the floor beside the couch. "After you took the kids back here last night, we all sat down and divvied up chores so you'll have time to take care of things for the kids. I'll help with them, but we all agreed you're working too hard. We're here to help.

If you check your texts, you'll see it all laid out."

RaeLynn didn't have to know Hunter very well to see the frustration on his face. He'd made it obvious that he didn't like asking for help and wanted to pull his own weight. But she was glad there were others making sure he didn't have to. She walked over and reached for the baby, who was also beginning to stir.

"Let me take her for a bit. We've become good friends. Whatever Wanda made for breakfast smells delicious. Go grab some before all the kids get up."

Bella immediately snuggled up to RaeLynn, and while RaeLynn remained firm on the idea that she was never having children, she had to admit it felt nice having a baby in her arms again.

Hunter walked over to the kitchen, where Wanda was already brewing coffee. "You just sit right down there, and

I'll have some of this black gold for you in no time."

The smile Hunter gave Wanda made RaeLynn's heart melt yet again. In so many ways, he was exactly the sort of man she would have liked for herself. Kind, generous, hardworking and always looking out for others. But while she appreciated all these qualities about him, and she didn't mind helping with the children for the short term, RaeLynn was not about to get herself involved with another set of responsibilities.

The baby needed changing, and for that, RaeLynn was glad. Not only did it mean Bella was feeling better, but it also gave her a break from thinking about Hunter in a totally inappropriate way. She changed the baby's diaper, then brought her back to the kitchen to make her a bottle. With Bella in her arms, greedily drinking her breakfast, RaeLynn sat at the kitchen table.

"You wouldn't mind dishing me up some of that, would you?" she asked Wanda. "My mouth has been watering ever since I carried it in."

"I was hoping to make you something a little bit nicer," Wanda said.

RaeLynn shook her head. "I keep telling you guys that I don't need fancy. I'm perfectly happy with everything you've done for me. What I've already come to love about the place is how you look out for everyone. I'm sure all of your guests feel very welcome, and the community spirit that you're exhibiting is exactly the kind of thing I want to write about. People forget about the value and beauty of helping each other in a time of need. It would have been so easy for you guys to let social services put the kids in foster care. But instead, you're coming together to keep their family intact."

"I am her family," Hunter said. "Just

because my wife died doesn't make her family less important to me."

Lynzee came out of the bedroom in her nightgown, carrying a faded baby blanket. "Why are all these people here?"

Hunter held an arm out to his daughter, who ran to him and gave him a giant hug.

"Wanda and Janie wanted to bring us some breakfast. You remember RaeLynn. She just came to say hi and have some breakfast with us."

Lynzee looked around the room. "You never bring us breakfast. We go to the ranch house to eat it."

She was a smart one, and RaeLynn could see how the little girl kept everyone on their toes.

Wanda brought a plate over to the table. "Well, today we brought it to you. Come eat before it gets cold."

Lynzee did as she was told, and just

as she was getting comfortable, Phoebe came out of the room.

"Tucker's up," she said.

Both RaeLynn and Hunter moved to get the little boy, but Janie was already in motion.

"You two sit. I've got this."

Funny how old habits died hard. RaeLynn would never have thought she'd be in some stranger's house jumping to take care of kids, but it was almost an automatic thing for her.

It was also funny that while she barely knew Hunter, he didn't feel like much of a stranger anymore. She couldn't help smiling at the way he coaxed Phoebe to try a bite of her breakfast, all while keeping an arm protectively around his daughter as she sat on his lap.

She hadn't known men like Hunter existed.

Janie brought Tucker into the kitchen, and as they all gathered together to share breakfast, it brought a strange longing to RaeLynn's heart.

She'd been telling herself all this time that she was fine without her family and didn't need them, that she was too busy to miss them. But suddenly, the story she'd been telling herself no longer felt like the truth.

Yes, it had been hard having so much on her shoulders. But as she looked down at the sweet baby nestled in her arms, she remembered moments like this as she'd held her sisters' babies and felt content in the midst of chaos. Of course, that peaceful feeling had never usually lasted long. So far, this little one seemed perfectly satisfied. And Rae-Lynn felt herself smiling from a deep place of contentment as she watched the kids chattering.

When they finished breakfast, Wanda set about putting the kitchen to rights while Janie took the kids to get them changed and dressed.

"We're going to take the kids over to the ranch house," Wanda said. "Hunter, you take RaeLynn around the ranch like you were supposed to do yesterday." She turned to RaeLynn. "I don't know what material you've been able to read through. I gave you all the guidebooks and maps and information we have, but if there's anything in particular you want to see, you just tell Hunter. There's only one person that knows the ranch better than Hunter, and that's Ricky. You'll meet him tonight at dinner."

Oh goody. With everything that had happened since she'd arrived, Rae-Lynn had forgotten why she originally hadn't wanted to come. The last thing she wanted was to talk to Ricky, but no story about the ranch would be complete without it.

"Sounds nice," RaeLynn said.

Hunter turned to Wanda. "Are you sure taking all the kids isn't an imposition?"

"You aren't so big that I can't give you a time-out, young man," she said. "Lynzee will finally have someone her own age to play with, so she won't drive Sam nuts. We have it all taken care of. Between me, Grace and Janie, we can handle six kids. That's one for each arm. Now, if we had more kids than we have arms, we might be in trouble."

Wanda laughed, and RaeLynn couldn't help laughing along with her. Her laughter quickly died down as she realized she'd never had this kind of support growing up. While these people were being helpful now, they obviously hadn't been around when her dad had died. From what her mom had told her, Ricky hadn't been supportive. In some ways, seeing this only made her resent her childhood even more.

The children came running out of the bathroom, freshly dressed and washed, looking excited to start their day.

"Janie is going to take your truck, Hunter, since all the car seats for Sadie's kids are already in it. We can stick Lynzee's car seat in mine," Wanda said. "Who would've thought that big old truck wouldn't be big enough to hold a passel of kids?"

Wanda chuckled, and they all went to load the kids up. Once the two trucks pulled out, Hunter turned to RaeLynn. "I know you said you're fine with all this, but I have to give you credit. Most people would've run away."

RaeLynn smiled at him. "I'm not most people," she said.

A wide grin split his face. "You certainly aren't."

Oh no. Was he flirting with her?

RaeLynn pushed her hair behind her ears, something to distract her, but then she realized it might be taken as her flirting back.

Great.

She did like him, wouldn't mind flirting with him, but what was the point of that? Everything about this situation was exactly what she didn't want for her life. While being here had reminded her to appreciate the things she'd left behind, it didn't mean she was going to invite them back into her life.

As sweet and cute as Hunter was, and as much as he seemed to be the kind of guy she'd like to get to know better, it didn't feel right to lead him on. She gestured out toward the rest of the ranch.

"Why don't you give me the grand tour you were planning, and then I can ask questions later?"

She made sure to use a professional tone, widening her stance so that she appeared all business. She didn't respond to his comment, and hopefully, he would take the hint.

Yes, she liked Hunter. More than she wanted to. But she wasn't going to act on it, because he was the last person on earth she could be with.

Chapter Three

Spending the day with RaeLynn was
supposed to be easy, but Hunter was
finding it mostly confusing. It wasn't
that she'd been rude or unfriendly or
anything like that. But there had been
unexpected moments where he'd felt a
connection to RaeLynn, and it seemed
like that made her feel uncomfortable.

Like now.

He'd brought her to the barn to check
out some new kittens that had recently
been born and needed homes. Something he'd do with any visitor. She sat

on a hay bale cuddling one of them and whispering things to it he couldn't hear. It wasn't the sort of thing he would usually find attractive, but he did. Just like when he'd seen her cuddling little Bella. RaeLynn might say she didn't want kids, but she was awfully good with them. More children needed mothers like her.

Hunter didn't want to be interested in someone like RaeLynn. He wasn't about to get involved with someone who didn't want the same things as him again. If he were going to remarry, it would have to be to someone who wanted to be a parent. Someone who loved the ranch as much as he did. And, God help him, as much as the past twenty-four hours had been insane, it would have to be someone who wanted more kids.

Becoming a father had been the best thing to ever happen to Hunter. And if he was going to bring another woman into his life, he needed her to feel the same way about becoming a mother. RaeLynn had said multiple times that she didn't want a family, and even though it didn't seem like she disliked life on the ranch, she didn't seem to love it, either.

That had been his mistake with Felicia. She'd talked about getting out, but he hadn't understood what that meant, or just how unhappy she'd been. Selfishly, Hunter had thought that in time she'd come to love it here. Unfortunately, that had never happened. And now, with Sadie in a similar situation, he understood the futility of trying to make someone live a life they didn't want.

He just didn't know how to do that with Sadie's situation. At least she had people to help her with the kids here. If she chased after the life she wanted in the city, who would help her? Who would be there if she went out drinking and messed up again?

Felicia used to tell him that she drank to forget about what an awful existence it was here. Would Sadie stop drinking if she lived somewhere else?

He didn't know.

That wasn't a problem he could solve now, but it would be worth discussing with her when he had the chance. She wasn't due in court until tomorrow, and while he knew he'd go there to support her, he didn't know what he was going to say.

But enough of that mess. He'd figure it out later.

He walked over to where RaeLynn was cuddling one of the kittens. "Seems like you've taken a shine to that little gray one," he said.

RaeLynn gave the kitten a kiss on his head and set it back down. "My friend had a cat who looked like this growing up. I loved that cat, and I was sad when my friend moved away. Funny, I missed the cat more than I missed her." She shook her head slowly. "I sound like a terrible person, don't I?"

Hunter sat on the bale next to her. "Not at all. Sometimes I think I like animals better than people. Why didn't you get a cat of your own?"

RaeLynn shrugged. "We were barely getting by as it was. There was no way we could've brought in a pet as well. And now—"

She looked thoughtful for a moment and then said, "I guess there's no reason why I couldn't get a cat. Maybe I'll go to the animal shelter and see what they have when I get home."

He gestured at the kitten she'd just put down. "Or you could take that one home. Looking for a home for these little critters is on my list of things to do. We didn't realize their mama was expecting when we got her from the Humane Society, so now instead of just one cat for the barn, we have more than we can handle."

"Really?" Her face lit up. "Are you sure? Wouldn't it miss its mother?"

Hunter picked up the kitten she'd set down and handed it back to her. "It's going to miss its mother whether it goes home with you or someone else. Personally, I'd like to see it go somewhere where I'm sure it's going to be loved."

She took the kitten and held it close to her. "I really do like him," she said. "He reminds me a little of a T. rex. I could call him Rex."

Yes, she was going to take the cat home. The way RaeLynn's face lit up when she named the little guy proved this kitten was meant for her.

"I think that settles it," he said. "Rex can stay in the barn with his family for now, but when you leave, he'll go home with you."

For a moment, RaeLynn looked like she was going to refuse, but then she smiled. "Funny how you don't realize just how much you want something until it's actually happening."

She set the kitten down and gave Hunter a quick hug. "Thank you."

Though the contact was brief, Hunter could still feel the warmth of her arms around him. He'd never wanted for hugs, not with how everyone at the ranch was like family. But that quick contact with RaeLynn was like downing a glass of water when you hadn't even realized you were thirsty.

RaeLynn was someone special. It seemed mighty unfair that the woman he was starting to have feelings for was all wrong for him and the life he loved. He'd promised himself he would never be in this kind of situation again, and yet here he was. Why was he only attracted to the kind of woman he couldn't be with?

He gestured toward the barn door. "We should probably get a move on. I still have lots to show you, and Ricky will be disappointed if I miss anything."

A strange look crossed her face. "He sounds like a tough taskmaster."

Hunter shrugged. "I guess you could say that. But you've got to be tough for life on the ranch. It's not all snuggling kittens and petting horses."

He led her out of the barn toward the trail to the lake. Everyone loved the exceptional views at the lake. It was beautiful, but there was a practical reason for the trail's location, too.

"Everyone loves this hiking trail because of how wide and easy it is to navigate. The reason it's so clear is because it used to be the main route for getting our cattle from the summer to the winter grazing grounds. Nowadays, moving the herd isn't that difficult. But it used to be a large and dangerous operation."

They made it to the first overlook, which had a clear view of the water. "The lake is man-made. About fifty years ago, they were moving the cattle along this trail, and a flash flood came and killed about a dozen of the hands as well as a good portion of the herd."

He gestured at the bench that sat facing the body of water. "It's not much, but it's a memorial to all those who lost their lives that day. There used to be a plaque, but it got faded with the weather, so it's being repaired. Water is scarce up here, so Ricky and his father hired an engineer to help channel where the floodwaters went and created the lake."

He looked over RaeLynn, who seemed to be studying the area intently. He knew it was her job to be interested in everything so she could write a good story, but there was sincerity to her that made him wonder if this was about more than writing a story.

Could he make her fall in love with the ranch?

It was stupid of him to think that he could make anyone change. He'd already learned that lesson the hard way. But he'd also never seen that level of interest from someone before.

"It's sad to think of all those lives lost," she said. "You'd never think that something so beautiful could be the site of such a tragedy."

"If it makes you feel any better, this isn't where they died. The lake is just something they built to make sure it never happens again. But there are no guarantees in ranching. The Double R was fortunate the fire didn't devastate us the way it did much of the town.

We're all very aware that we can't control nature, and we're always mindful of the potential danger."

She looked slightly relieved by his words, though it didn't seem to erase the furrows in her brow.

"Everything okay?" he asked.

She shrugged. "It's just sad that all there is to show for the tragedy is a plaque that's being repaired."

"I can understand that," he said. "My uncle Vern was one of the men who died. I never knew him, but my family says the Double R went out of their way to do the right thing by the people who lost their loved ones. There is an actual memorial, but the families wanted to keep it private, because at the time of the incident, there was a lot of media attention, and the grieving families didn't want to be a sideshow. I guess it's been long enough that the people who were most hurt by it are gone now, so I can show you if you like?"

RaeLynn nodded, but uncertainty was written all over her face.

"If it makes you uncomfortable, we can head back."

He took her down the trail a ways until they got to the gate that blocked off the path to the memorial.

"They keep it closed off so the public doesn't wander in. It's important to Ricky to respect the privacy of the affected families."

Her expression softened a little, but something about her demeanor still seemed off. She didn't say anything, though, and something told him that he'd be intruding if he commented on it.

The memorial site also had a nice view of the lake. In his opinion, it was the best view. It just seemed wrong to say so, given how somber RaeLynn was. Her audible gasp when they got to the memorial didn't surprise him. Most people reacted that way when they saw the amount of effort that had gone into creating this place.

Hunter gestured at the bench that stood in the middle of the memorial stones. "You can sit there if you like. No one's really supposed to know, but Ricky frequently comes here to pray. He was raised to believe that showing emotion is a sign of weakness, and even though he's gotten a lot better about it, he still keeps things like this private."

She walked around the ring of stones. The memorial had been designed as a circle of markers for those who had died.

"I know they look like gravestones, but no one is buried here. The families were all given the bodies to honor in their own way, but the Ruiz family wanted to create a memorial of their own. The families are all welcome to come and pay their respects as they wish."

"Why the circle?"

"Because the love for our family is unbroken."

He walked over to the marker for his uncle. "Uncle Vern didn't have any kids, but my mom used to tell us about him and made sure we paid our respects. I would've liked to have met the guy. My mom's stories about him always cracked me up."

"What about the bodies that weren't found?"

That was something not a lot of people knew about. "You must have really done your homework. Here I was thinking I was telling you something new about the ranch, but you already know about this stuff."

She gave him a small smile. "That's my job. But I like to hear other people's versions, because you never know what interesting tidbits you'll find that weren't part of the original write-ups."

He hadn't thought of it that way, but again, it was one more thing for him to appreciate about RaeLynn. Not only was she thorough but she hadn't made him feel like he was wasting her time with his stories.

"Over here," Hunter said. He indicated the relevant stones. "Only two were never found. This guy here, Paul Gentry, was apparently my uncle's best friend. Last time my mom was here visiting, she and Ricky were up half the night laughing at stories about all the trouble they got into."

Her face softened slightly as he talked. "I didn't realize that your mom was the same age as Ricky. He seems like he'd be more of the age to be your grandfather."

Hunter laughed. "I was one of those late-in-life surprise babies. My mother thought she couldn't have children, so boy, were they surprised when I came along."

He smiled at RaeLynn. "It's why my mom always tells me to never count God out. God can do some amazing things, and just because it doesn't happen according to our timeline doesn't mean it won't work out."

She walked over to the bench and wrapped her arms around herself, like she was cold, even though it was a warm day.

"It's so weird to hear how everyone at the ranch talks about God as though He's a real person they have a relationship with. Don't get me wrong, I believe in God and all that, but what you guys believe seems to be different."

He sat on the bench next to her. "I can understand that. I spent my whole life going to church, but God didn't become a real person to me until I realized just how hard life is without Him."

She stared at him for a moment. "How does He make it easier? It's not like He does anything for you. He can't watch all those kids for you."

"True," he said. "But He did bring some amazing people into my life who can help. But it's more than just that. When I feel most alone, I know that He's there. I can talk to Him. And I don't feel so alone anymore."

Hunter looked over at her. "But maybe you don't feel that way ever, so you don't need it."

"I feel that way a lot," she said. "It just never occurred to me that God could help with something like that."

He took a deep breath. Talking about this kind of stuff was never his strong suit. But hopefully, with a quick prayer to God for assistance, he would find the right words.

"You seem kind of sad since we started talking about the tragedy. I don't want to pry, so if you don't want to talk about it with me, you could tell God what's in your heart."

RaeLynn nodded slowly. "I guess I could do that," she said. "And thank you for recognizing that I'm dealing with something I need to keep private."

She sat on the grass and closed her eyes. Maybe it was intrusive of him, but he watched her face for a moment, noticing that she appeared to be deep in prayer. When a tear rolled down her cheek, he stepped away, hoping to give her some privacy.

He said his own prayer that God would help her deal with whatever she was going through, but as he stole one last look at her, he also asked God to help him with these feelings he was having for her. He liked RaeLynn. Found her attractive in so many ways. But there were way too many reasons why a relationship with her wouldn't work.

Coming here wasn't supposed to have affected her this way. RaeLynn hadn't expected to feel such a connection to this place. She didn't know why she'd gone and asked about the people whose bodies had never been found. Her mother had told her about it, and how it was one more reason not to trust the people on the Double R. In her mother's version of the story, the Double R hadn't done anything for the families of the victims, and the flood had just been an excuse to create the lake that had ended up diverting the water from the smaller ranches and put them out of business.

She looked out over the lake. Her mom had told her that the Double R had driven their family out of business when they'd created the lake. It had been a shady deal, but because the Double R had fancy lawyers, small ranches like her grandfather's had gone under.

RaeLynn had done some research, and over the years there had been a few challenges to the Double R's water rights, but the Double R had always won. As a journalist, she knew there were multiple sides to every story, and only after hearing all of them did you approach something close to the truth.

So what was the truth about the Double R?

RaeLynn had to write something positive and encouraging because that was the mission of her magazine. But for her own peace of mind, understanding the dark secrets hidden there was important.

RaeLynn's mother had been disowned by her family for marrying RaeLynn's father, Cinco. When Cinco died, RaeLynn's mother had been left on her own to figure out what do with a baby on the way. Even though RaeLynn didn't fully agree with the choices her mother had made, she wasn't sure she could have done any better.

She glanced at the memorial stones. Her mother had told her that the Double R didn't care about their people. But these well-tended markers, some fifty years later, said the opposite.

She took a deep breath. *God, I don't know if what Hunter says about the Double R is true. I know he has a bias. But I have one, too, and I'm just trying to figure out the truth.*

Saying the words, even just in her head, did make her feel slightly better. But it wasn't like there were any answers, either. Hopefully, her time here would give her some clarity. She'd been prepared to write a positive article about her enemy, but what did it mean when the person you thought was your enemy seemed like a good guy?

She wiped the tears from her eyes. She wasn't usually an emotional person, and she certainly didn't get emotional over a story. She'd always prided herself on her objectivity.

Hunter handed her a bandanna. "Sorry, it's nothing fancy, but it'll do the trick."

She looked down at it, and while it was a simple gesture, the thoughtfulness behind it touched her heart. Sure, he'd probably do the same for anyone else, but she wasn't used to someone being so thoughtful. And she certainly wasn't used to getting attached to the subject of a story so quickly. Yes, she'd liked many of the people she'd done stories on. But this was different. If so much weren't riding on her doing a good job with this one, RaeLynn would be tempted to walk away or, at the very least, assign this to someone else.

"Thank you," she said. "You must think it's strange I'm getting all teared up over people I didn't even know." She wanted to apologize for being unprofessional, but the sincerity on Hunter's face made her realize he'd probably be insulted.

Hunter shrugged. "It's not for me to judge. You feel what you feel."

Though she absolutely believed that was true, it was strange hearing it from someone else. Maybe it was silly of her, but the acceptance she found in his small kindness was more than she'd felt in a long time. The tenderness on Hunter's face made her realize that he actually cared. And while she was used to small-town hospitality, this felt more like friendship.

Maybe that was the stupidest emotion of them all. RaeLynn didn't make friends with her subjects. She barely had friends beyond casual acquaintances. She'd always been so busy helping her family and working hard to make a life for herself that she'd never had the time or the energy. Plus, people got offended when you had to cancel plans with them because your sister dropped off her kid for you to watch again.

Even though Hunter had respectfully stepped away, she still felt like she owed him something in return. A piece of herself, since he'd let her in.

"My mom grew up on a ranch," she said.

Explaining to him how different this experience was from what she'd been expecting would be a good place to start, but she also wasn't going to tell him everything.

"The way she made it sound…" Rae-Lynn continued. "She said the big ranchers were all about profit, and they didn't care about the people. She spoke of ranch life with such bitterness that I've never had a very positive view of ranching."

"We're family," Hunter said. "I know that doesn't always mean much to people these days, but we take care of our own. Always have, always will."

She wanted to ask why they hadn't taken care of her mom or her. But she knew the answer already. Her mom had made the decision to leave. She hadn't wanted RaeLynn to grow up in such a controlling environment. But so far, RaeLynn hadn't seen that kind of attitude. Then again, she'd just gotten here, and everyone was being on their best behavior.

She stood and brushed the dirt off her jeans. "I can see why everyone loves it here so much," she said.

"Would you like to walk farther down

the trail, or have you had enough for today?" he asked.

Again, she was touched by his kindness and thoughtfulness toward her. Hunter had a way of making her feel like he cared about her.

"I would like to see the lake up close," she said. "I understand there's great fishing."

"You fish?"

RaeLynn laughed at the surprised note in his voice. "I don't look the type?"

Hunter laughed with her. "That was probably a dumb thing for me to say. You seem to be good at so many things, so it's unbelievable there's one more to add to the list. I mean that in a good way."

It was kind of cute how he seemed embarrassed at complimenting her.

RaeLynn smiled at him. "I do like to fish. I haven't done it since I was a kid, but I really enjoyed it. I've often wished for the opportunity to do so again, but life gets busy, and I'd need all the equipment."

He took his hat off, running his fingers through his hair, and then set it back on his head. "I know all about that," he said. "I love to fish, but it seems like every time I take Lynzee out, work interrupts."

"What keeps you so busy at the ranch?" she said.

Hunter grinned. "What doesn't keep me busy? Everyone has their jobs, and I check to make sure everything is running smoothly, and when it's not, I step in and make sure the job gets done right."

The intensity on his face made her smile. "You sound like there's a bit of a control freak in you," she said.

"I guess I do. I think it's because I know the importance of safety and doing things right. I'm responsible for the welfare of our animals but also of the people on this ranch. I take that responsibility very seriously. If mistakes are made, people could get hurt or even die."

She didn't doubt it. Knowing he paid such attention to everyone's safety made her feel just a little bit better.

They continued down the trail, and it felt good to be out in nature. She could see the appeal of living in a place like this. She liked how her work allowed her to help support small towns and their communities. She got to see the beauty many people missed and hopefully share the value of that beauty with others.

As they reached the lake, RaeLynn saw an older man fishing off the dock.

When they were within range, Hunter said, "Ricky! Look who I brought."

Oh no. No. Just no. She was not ready for this. She'd thought she'd gotten to the point where she was open to the idea of getting to know Ricky. But she was not ready to come face-to-face with him in reality.

Hunter seemed to sense her hesitation. "It's okay. He doesn't bite. Ricky gets along with everyone. Just a few minutes of conversation and you'll feel like you've known him forever."

As they got closer, RaeLynn tried to do some quick breathing exercises to calm her nerves. She'd once interviewed the governor of Colorado and hadn't been this nervous. What if he was everything her mother had warned her he was? And what if, like so much of what she'd experienced on the ranch, he wasn't like she expected?

As Ricky walked toward her, he looked like any other old-timer she'd encountered in other small towns in Colorado. He had the look of a man who'd lived a long life and had tales that would make a great book someday.

There was a light and warmth in his eyes, and as much as she hated to admit it, he was the kind of man she would usually want to sit and talk to for hours. People like him always had the best stories. But the one she wanted to know the most was why he'd driven her parents away. And why he had made her mother so scared after her father had died.

"It's such a pleasure to meet you," Ricky said. "I'm sorry I didn't get the chance to last night, but with all the commotion with Sadie's kids, we were shorthanded, and I needed to pitch in."

He glanced over at Hunter. "And don't you be giving me any of your nonsense about it. As long as there's still air in my lungs, I can still pull my own weight on my ranch."

Her mom had said that Ricky was one

of the hardest-working men she'd ever known. And this proved it. Clearly, her mom hadn't been wrong about everything.

"I appreciate it," Hunter said. "It looks like Pretty Little Lady is about to foal."

Ricky grinned. "I just checked on her before I came out here." He looked over at RaeLynn. "Have you ever seen a baby horse being born?"

RaeLynn nodded. "I have. I got to do an article on High Meadow Farms, and I just happened to be there when one of their foals was born. It's a beautiful sight. I can see why you enjoy being part of it."

Ricky grinned. "I made a big investment in the horses, so I like to make sure everything is taken care of."

One more thing that sounded a lot like the Ricky her mother had told her about. The way Hunter and Ricky grinned at each other, RaeLynn was pretty sure they were both cut from the same cloth. She'd observed some places where Hunter liked to have control, and she could understand why. But what she couldn't understand was why Ricky had been so controlling of her parents.

"Now, tell me what you all saw today," Ricky said, looking from Hunter to RaeLynn.

"We just got back from seeing the memorial for the people who died in the flood," RaeLynn said.

Ricky scowled over at Hunter and then turned his attention back to Rae-Lynn. "I don't want that made into a circus. Good men died that day, and I don't want to profit off it."

There was more of that compassion RaeLynn hadn't thought Ricky had.

"I won't include it," she promised. "I thought it was nice that you had made such a good memorial for them."

Ricky took off his hat and held it in

his hands. "I only wish I could've done more. We did our best to do right by all the families, but it always feels like it's not enough. What price can you put on a man's life?"

In her mother's version of the story, people had been cheated badly. But the sadness and remorse on Ricky's face spoke of a man who would never cheat others. Her mother had told her to be wary of Ricky because he was good at manipulating people. In all the interviews she'd done, RaeLynn had met a lot of manipulators. Ricky seemed sincere.

Was she failing to be objective, or was it possible that her mother hadn't been objective?

She smiled at Ricky. "I imagine you do have some regrets after all your years ranching, but it sounds like you've tried to do the right thing."

He looked down at the hat he hadn't

put back on. "I have more than my share, and they're all my own fault. My biggest regret was fighting with my son, Cinco, and not supporting his rodeo dreams. I was worried he'd be hurt or killed by some bull, and I was right. It's not the 'I told you so' I ever wanted to have to say."

He looked up at her with sad eyes that spoke of great tragedy. He couldn't possibly know who she was. Her mother had made sure of it, and RaeLynn wasn't going to put her DNA information out in one of those genealogy websites, like Ricky's other grandchildren had done.

"I'm sorry for your loss," she said.

Ricky shook his head. "I don't want your sympathy. But I would like you to put something in that magazine of yours showing my apology for what happened with my son. Cinco's wife disappeared while expecting a baby, and I don't know anything about that baby. Or how they fared in life. I pray every day that they're okay."

RaeLynn's chest squeezed so tightly that she wasn't sure she could breathe. She'd heard about Ricky's search for her, but she'd always figured it was some kind of publicity thing. But hearing him and his longing did something funny to her heart.

"I understand you've found other children fathered by Cinco," she said. "It sounds like you have a very full family life. Surely they bring you joy?"

Ricky set his hat back on his head and gestured toward the dock. "Come fish with me for a bit. I think better when I'm doing something."

She couldn't say no. She'd just told Hunter about her longing to go fishing again. The weird thing was, as much as she didn't want to interact with this man, she thought about all the times growing up that she'd been envious of her friends fishing with their grandfathers.

So this was it. She was going fishing with hers. He didn't know who she was, and she wasn't sure she wanted him to. She wasn't sure her heart would be able to take the conflicting emotions if she spent so much time with him.

"You want me to give you some privacy?" Hunter asked.

No. She couldn't be alone with this man. Not with these feelings jumbled up inside her. What if she couldn't take it anymore and confessed everything?

RaeLynn looked over at him. "Please stay. We were just talking about how much we both wished we could fish more. Plus, I love the interaction between the two of you. It will help me with my article."

The smile Hunter gave her was probably just supposed to make her feel better about the situation. But the content expression on his face told her that inviting him to stay might have been yet another mistake.

Now her heart was in danger not just from one man but two.

Chapter Four

The news coming out of the courthouse on Monday wasn't good. At least not for Sadie. While Hunter had expected to have to take care of the children for an extended period of time, this had only solidified how long that might be. Sadie would be in jail until her trial, which wouldn't be for at least another month. Because she was a repeat offender, the DA was going to make sure she spent a lot of time in jail.

"Hunter," Eleanor said, standing before him, "you have to be reasonable.

You're not equipped for foster care, and you and I both know this isn't going to be a short-term deal. The DA is pushing for the maximum sentence, and given her record, she's going to get it. She'll be in jail a few months, and when she gets out, she'll have to get a job, create a home, and prove that she's capable of raising these children. We're not looking at a couple of weeks, not even a couple of months. It'll likely be at least a year. Are you really able to make that kind of commitment?"

A year. Eleanor was right. He'd thought it would be a few weeks and, depending on what her sentence was, maybe months. As much as he wanted to believe otherwise, it wasn't unreasonable to think she would need even more time to get on her feet, especially with the way social services had been looking at her already.

But this was family. That meant he was going to be there for them.

"I understand all that," he said. "If it's going to be that amount of time, these kids need to be with their family more than ever. They need stability. What's more stable than living with the uncle they've always known and had in their lives? It's sure better than a bunch of strangers, especially if they're split up."

He looked over at where RaeLynn was cuddling the baby as she watched the children on the playground. They'd come to meet up with Eleanor at the park after the hearing.

"Bella is just a baby," he continued. "She's not going to know her mom when she gets out, and if you put her with this family who wants a baby but not the other kids, her siblings are going to be strangers as well. We both know this is the best chance to keep everyone together, so you tell me what I need to do, and I'll do it."

She sighed, like she'd expected his answer and didn't like it. "Typically, you have to go through classes to be certified as a foster parent. I can give you the materials and waive that condition, but you're still going to have to meet all the other requirements set forth by the county. I can give you some time to get things in order. But you need to understand that if something goes wrong, I'm liable. And it's not just my job I'm worried about but the kids. I know you think I'm being a hardnose here, but their safety is my top priority. Watching them for a few days is easy for you, but how is it going to work for the next few months? How will you balance your job and your other responsibilities with taking care of them as well as being a father to your own daughter? You're about to go from being a single father to one child to a single father to four, including a baby."

Hunter took a deep breath. These were all things he'd thought of on his own. Having her say them out loud only made them more real. What if he couldn't handle it? Would he be in over his head? Everyone at the Double R had been extremely helpful. Ricky had even let him use one of the ranch SUVs to come into town so that he had enough room for all the kids in their car seats. Everyone else at the ranch was chipping in to help him out on a temporary basis, but would they still be willing if they knew this was going to be a more permanent commitment than they'd all thought at first?

It didn't matter. He'd make it work. He had to.

"I know it's going to be an adjustment," he said. "Even though it's just me on my own, I have a good support system. You know that."

Lynzee's laugh rang out across the playground, and he looked over to see RaeLynn playing some kind of chasing game with the kids, and they all were laughing.

"How long is she sticking around?" the social worker asked. "She's giving you a lot of help now, but what happens when she leaves? I understand she's just here to write an article."

He'd admit that was part of the trouble. RaeLynn had helped him a lot over the weekend, and he appreciated it. But her stay was temporary, and he was going to have to learn how to do all this on his own.

"You know I have the others at the ranch as well."

She nodded. "I know. I just don't think you understand what a big job you're setting yourself up for. I'm going to need to run background checks on everyone you have taking care of the children, and you're still going to have to do all the other things we require of our foster parents."

He'd read all the paperwork she'd given him, but as she explained the further requirements of the situation, his heart sank. It did feel like a daunting task, mostly because it seemed like the kids would be taken away from him if he made the smallest mistake.

"Whatever it takes," he said. He meant it. He already felt like he'd gone above and beyond to make sure the kids were his first priority. He'd accepted more help in the past few days than he had since coming to the Double R. Even in the days after Felicia's death, when he was alone and figuring out how to be a dad on his own while grieving the loss of his wife, he hadn't accepted this much help. But he'd swallowed his pride now and would continue doing so if that's what it took to keep the children together.

Eleanor seemed to accept that she wasn't going to change his mind with this one conversation.

"Very well, then. I'll get started on the rest of the paperwork, and I'll be by the ranch later this week to get everyone who will be caring for the children to consent to the background checks. Please don't make me regret this."

When he finished going over the rest of the paperwork and giving the necessary signatures, he walked back over to the park. As soon as he crossed to the playground space, the kids stopped what they were doing and ran over to him.

"Daddy!" Lynzee ran to him and threw her arms around his leg, giving him a big hug.

Before he could scoop her up and

hold her tightly against him, Phoebe was right there, hugging his other leg. "Uncle Daddy!"

He chuckled at the nickname. He'd always been Uncle Hunter to them. But since this morning, Phoebe had started calling him Uncle Daddy. It was probably because of Lynzee, but he also thought the little girl longed for a father of her own.

The last conversation he'd had with Sadie about her kids was how much they needed a father figure in their lives. He'd done his best to provide that, considering none of their fathers had ever stuck around. Eleanor had told him that she was legally bound to reach out to the men. She'd done so in one of her earlier investigations, but they'd all indicated they didn't want any involvement with the children.

She'd have to contact them again, given the change in Sadie's circumstances, but he already knew what their answers would be. It was a shame Sadie hadn't known how to pick a guy, because these kids deserved better. But as long as he was around, he'd make sure they had what they needed.

He bent to hug both little girls close to him, and Tucker ran up as well, his babbling completely indistinguishable. Even though some people might say it was strange to be excited about baby talk, it was more than what the child usually said. Since coming to Hunter's, the little guy was babbling more, trying out words and sounds, and it warmed his heart to see how the boy seemed to be thriving.

A pang of guilt hit him at that thought. He wasn't trying to replace their mother or say that she'd been doing a bad job. Maybe she hadn't been doing the best by them, but she'd been trying. And he knew that she loved them. He just hoped that suffering the consequences of her actions would finally open her eyes to what she needed to be doing with her life.

"How'd it go?" RaeLynn asked, smiling at him as she untangled her hair from the baby's hand.

"Good, I guess," he said. "It looks like I'm going to have the kids for a year or so, based on what the social worker said. I wasn't expecting it to be that long, but what else am I going to do?"

"Daddy, watch me slide," Lynzee said, pulling away and running back toward the playground with the other two children trailing after her. He smiled at his little girl's enthusiasm and the happy way her cousins followed her. He couldn't remember the last time they'd gone to the playground on a Monday in the middle of the day like this. They usually went in the evening or on weekends. He always felt so pressured for time because of everything he needed to get done.

Ricky had told him to take today off, partially to deal with the legal mess with Sadie but also to show RaeLynn around town. RaeLynn thought it would be fun to do so with the children. That way she could put a family angle in her article, showing everyone what a family-friendly place Columbine Springs was.

The fire that had ravaged the town almost two years ago had burned the old playground. But thanks to various donors and the fundraising efforts of Janie and Alexander, a new playground had been built in its place. Hunter had to admit it was better than the one that had been destroyed.

A family he knew from church arrived at the playground, and Hunter gave them a wave. They waved back, letting their children loose on the equipment as well. The Riverfront Park had always been a place where families gathered, and it was the site of many town events. It looked different now with so many of the trees and old structures burned. But small pieces had been salvaged and combined with the new things that had been added, and Hunter felt hope for their future.

Maybe that's what this situation with Sadie was for him. A fire in his personal life that he could rebuild upon and create something new for all of them on.

RaeLynn shifted the baby to her other side, and Hunter held his arms out to her. "I'm sure she's getting heavy. Let me have a turn."

RaeLynn looked like she was going to protest, but she handed him the baby. Bella wriggled in his arms like she wanted to get down and play, and RaeLynn laughed.

"I know she's not quite old enough to be mobile yet, but with the way she wants to be with the others, I'm sure she'll start everything early."

Hunter laughed as he adjusted his grip on her. "I've noticed. It's nice to see the others try to play with her and bring her along when they can. Phoebe is especially always making sure that Bella is included."

RaeLynn nodded slowly. "I'm sure Phoebe is almost like a surrogate mother to her. I see all the things that she does with Bella, and I'm sure it's because her mom has asked her to help."

The pain in her eyes told him she was talking from her experience.

"She does seem to know a lot more than most four-year-olds about taking care of a baby," he said.

"Being around Lynzee is good for her because she gets to be a kid. When we first got to the park, Phoebe hovered over Bella like she thought she was expected to help watch her. I can't forget the relief on her face when I shooed her away to go enjoy herself."

Hunter sighed. "Someone so young shouldn't feel that responsibility."

"Exactly," RaeLynn said. "But going back to what you said earlier, a year is a long time. Are you sure you're up for it?"

He glanced at the little girls who had started playing with the other children who'd arrived. The way they were laughing and smiling softened his heart in a funny way.

"I'd already made up my mind to do so," he said. "But what you told me about them solidifies my decision. Phoebe deserves to be a kid, not always watching out for her younger brother and sister."

"I appreciate your commitment," she

said. "Not a lot of people would do what you're doing."

He shrugged. "You did."

She nodded. "Yes, but I got out. Now I work very hard to avoid ever having to do it again."

Bella grabbed at his face, tugging at his nose. He jerked away, laughing. "With this little one, it's hard to have a conversation."

RaeLynn nodded. "Just remember that will be for the next year of your life." She glanced over to where the children were now playing at the sandbox. "And what happens if Sadie doesn't get her act together? What if she comes out of jail and falls back into her old ways? Are you prepared to make this a permanent change?"

Now that was a question he hadn't considered. He assumed Sadie would want to straighten up and be a good mother to her children, but RaeLynn had a point. What if Sadie didn't want to change? What if having all this time without her children made her want her freedom and old way of life even more?

He listened to the children's laughter and then looked back at RaeLynn. "If I let them go into the system, they'll be split up forever. Those three children would grow up without knowing each other, and Lynzee would grow up without them. That doesn't sound like a very good alternative. I'll do what I have to do."

RaeLynn looked thoughtful for a moment. Then she said, "I don't mean to be insensitive, but have you thought about what impact that could have on your personal life? If you wanted to date someone, three more kids would make it a lot harder."

He gave a small chuckle. "Dating? Sure, I've thought about it, but my daughter is my number one priority. It's hard to date with a child and a demanding job. I always wanted more children, so maybe this is God's way of making it happen."

RaeLynn gave a small shrug. "It's just a lot easier for a woman to accept one child instead of four."

The way she said it made him wonder about the times he'd thought she might have been getting slightly flirtatious with him. Was she talking about a hypothetical woman? Or was this about her?

He didn't know, but it was irrelevant. She'd made it clear she was leaving. And she'd also made it clear she didn't want children of her own or anyone else's to raise. That was a shame, because she was so good with them. He was enjoying his time with her, so this was something he needed to keep in mind, given the occasional romantic pang he felt for her.

It wasn't just that RaeLynn was pretty. They'd had all kinds of pretty women come to the ranch as guests, and none had turned his head the way she did. It was her openness of heart that drew him in and made him feel things he hadn't thought he could feel again.

He'd spoken about finding someone else, but it had always been in a more speculative way, not as something he'd ever actually expected to happen. He'd be lying if he said he wouldn't be interested in something happening with RaeLynn, but he liked her too much to put her in the uncomfortable position of having to consider taking on things she'd already said she didn't want in her life.

Anyway, all this conjecture about future relationships was too far away for him to think about. He didn't know if he was going to get to keep the kids. If he did get to keep them, he didn't know how long they would be with him. He also didn't know what was going to happen when Sadie got out of jail. And even if he knew the answers to all those unknowns, life had taught him that the things you think you can count on can so easily be gone in an instant. He would never have expected that Felicia would die so young, and here they were. He had to remember to take each day for what it was, plan for the future, but not so much that he'd be disappointed when those plans didn't work out.

Even as his mind was telling himself these things, he looked over at RaeLynn playing with Tucker, and his heart told him that he would be a fool to let her go.

What had she been thinking, asking Hunter about his dating life? It was none of her business, and she berated herself for the question multiple times over the next couple of days. It seemed she'd opened that can of worms, and even though she tried to firmly put the lid on it and any idea of Hunter dating, every once in a while, one of those worms would slither out and taunt her.

Like now. They'd just finished supper at the main ranch house, where they seemed to have most of their meals. Ricky was regaling them with tales of the old cowboy days, and RaeLynn knew she should probably be taking notes. So far, she hadn't seen signs of a temper in the charming old cowboy, nor had she seen any evidence of him being the hard man her mom had told her about.

After the wiry eighty-something-year-old man finished his story, he dropped to his hands and knees, and the children climbed on his back, calling him the horse. When she turned away, she caught Hunter looking at her with a wistful look on his face, like he wanted to join her and share in a personal moment of their own. The trouble was, she wanted it, too, even though she knew it was the wrong thing for both of them. What good would it do to talk to him, to deepen her relationship with him? It went against everything she'd planned for herself.

Wanda came into the room with a stern look on her face. "Enough with that tomfoolery. Ricky, you're too old for such nonsense."

The children climbed off Ricky's back, and he stood, shaking his head. "You're never too old to enjoy the company of young children and to encourage them in their passions."

"You can still encourage them," Wanda said, "but that doesn't mean you need to be their personal jungle gym."

Ricky laughed. "I've got to enjoy these little ones. I never got to enjoy my grandchildren when they were young."

A pang hit RaeLynn's stomach as she realized that he was talking about her, only he didn't know that. She'd have liked to have had a grandfather growing up, to have this interaction and to feel part of the family.

That was why she couldn't help but support Hunter's decision to keep the family together, even though she knew he had a long road ahead of him.

What would her life have been like had her mother not cut ties with Ricky? Her mom had always said they were better off that way, but watching Ricky with the children now made her feel like she'd missed out.

Hunter walked past her, giving her a smile. "Wanda's homemade ice cream is ready. Want to come with me and grab some so we can enjoy it before the children?"

The children were laughing at whatever faces Ricky was making at them, and with as many people as there were in the room, they were in capable hands.

Ricky didn't know it, but all of his grandchildren were gathered here on the ranch now. Rachel was back from her delayed honeymoon with her husband and daughter. Janie and Alexander and their son, Sam, were here, and so were Grace and William with their new baby. The baby was just slightly younger than Bella, and the two of them were on a blanket with a bunch of toys, playing as happily as young babies could together.

It was a picture-perfect evening with all the extended family gathered together. Had RaeLynn grown up here, she wouldn't have had Rachel, Alexander and William with her, since no one had known they existed until Ricky started his search for her. But with the number of ranch hands and staff who spent time here like they were family,

RaeLynn could still picture a similar upbringing for herself.

But she also loved the siblings that her mother had acquired for her along the way, and she wouldn't have them now if she'd grown up here. Still, to have had the kind of support that Hunter was getting now would have changed her life significantly, in a good way. She wouldn't have had to spend so much time raising her siblings and their children. There would have been help from adults. What would it have been like for RaeLynn to have had a childhood?

That was the gift Hunter was giving to Phoebe, even if he didn't understand how priceless it was. But it wasn't just Hunter changing the kids' lives. He had the help of the family, even if they weren't technically his family. He was just the ranch foreman. Although everyone said he was Ricky's right-hand man, he was still an employee. But you wouldn't know it by the love Ricky gave these children and the way everyone in Ricky's family went out of their way to support Hunter and take care of the kids.

This was the family life she'd always dreamed of. And when she walked out to the back deck for some of the homemade ice cream, the longing in her heart only deepened. One of her happy childhood memories was going to a new grandparent's cabin in the woods and eating homemade ice cream. She'd liked that family. The stepfather had also been pretty cool, except for the fact that six months after he and their mother got married, he went to jail on drug-trafficking charges. Funny how people weren't always what they seemed.

Maybe that was the lesson she needed to take away from all of this. Her mother had always told her that they didn't have a relationship with Ricky and his family because they were bad people. But maybe her mother's opinion was flawed. After all, she didn't have the best judgment in people. Could her mother have been wrong about Ricky all these years?

Rachel handed her a bowl of ice cream with the usual grace and contented smile she'd come to know from her sister. Sometimes she caught herself staring at her, wondering what it would have been like to have known her as a child. Rachel had grown up in the foster-care system. When she'd heard Hunter was doing all this to keep his nieces and nephew out of care, she'd eagerly stepped up to help. She wanted the children to know the family she'd never had.

While they'd had different family experiences, RaeLynn suspected that, growing up, they'd both felt a deep longing for family connection. Sometimes RaeLynn just wanted to tell Rachel they were sisters and build a relationship with her. But that felt like a betrayal of her mother and the siblings she'd grown up with.

The longer she was here, and the closer she got to everyone, the harder it would be to tell them the truth. Would they be angry with her because she'd taken so long to tell them who she was? Would they believe her? RaeLynn didn't know how to handle so many doubts and fears.

Hunter gestured at a porch swing on the corner of the deck. "Let's sit for a spell," he said. "I feel like all we've done lately is run, run, run. It will be nice to have a quiet moment to ourselves."

We. Ourselves. Like they'd already formed some kind of partnership. In a way, they had. And that made these feelings of unease even worse.

As if Rachel could sense RaeLynn's doubts, she gave her an encouraging smile. "It's okay. The kids will be fine. They'll all be out here in a few minutes clamoring for ice cream, and there are enough adults around that we can handle it. You've been working so hard. You deserve a break."

As much as she told herself and everyone else that her stay here was temporary, they all included her as if she were one of them. One more adopted member of their extended family, and none of them understood that she really was family. She followed Hunter over to the swing and when they sat, peace fell over her.

What if she didn't leave?

An irrational question, considering she had other responsibilities. Instead of sitting here on a swing eating ice cream with a handsome cowboy, she should be in her cabin working on her article. She'd written a lot, but none of it seemed right. She'd finish a section, think it good and then realize it was too long. But when she cut it, she felt like she was missing so many important details that people needed to know about the ranch. About the community.

She'd written about so many different ranching businesses, towns and colorful characters, but none had wormed their way into her heart the way the Double R and Columbine Springs had. She'd moved around so much growing up that it been hard to get a sense of home. Being here felt like home in such an inexplicable way that it was hard to imagine living anywhere else.

That was ridiculous, though. She had a job to do. And when her time here was over, her article finished, she'd be back in Denver saving a magazine that people desperately needed.

"Your ice cream is going to melt," Hunter said.

She looked down at her bowl. "It seems too pretty to eat."

He smiled at her. "But it's meant to be eaten, so you might as well enjoy it while it's still cold and delicious."

They ate the ice cream in silence, and it was as delicious as it looked. She could sense Hunter relaxing beside her, and as she stole a glance at him, she could see the peace settling over his face. This was probably the first actual break he'd gotten since the children had come to live with him.

People helped with the children during the day, but she knew he was wrestling with them alone all night. He'd admitted the baby didn't sleep very well, except for when they were on the recliner together with her lying on his chest. But that didn't let him sleep very well because he was afraid she'd move and fall off.

Part of her wanted to offer to take the baby one night so he could just get some sleep, but she knew he had to figure this out on his own. She'd be gone soon.

The sound of children's laughter broke the silence. "It was so nice and quiet," Hunter said.

"It was peaceful out here," she said.

Further ending the quiet and the mood was a beep from Hunter's cell phone. He pulled it out and checked the text.

"One of the horses has been acting a little colicky over the past few hours," he said. "A ranch hand just texted me to see if I could come give him a break from walking her. The vet is on the way, so it shouldn't be long. But I do need to be there. Our head trainer, Fernando, would usually do this, but he's on vacation with his wife and baby. You don't have to come, but it might be interesting to see another aspect of ranch life."

RaeLynn nodded. Over the years, many of the ranchers she'd talked to had mentioned colic and how it impacted horses, but she'd never seen it for herself.

"As long as you don't think I'll be in the way. I would like to see as many aspects of ranch life as I can."

They brought the bowls back over to the table where Rachel was still dishing out the dessert. "Thunder is still colicky. Steve asked me to come relieve him for a bit until the vet gets here, and I should be there for the vet anyway. Do you mind looking out for the kids while I'm gone?"

Rachel smiled at him. "Of course not."

She glanced at her watch. "I imagine it will be a while," she said. "Once we finish up with the ice cream, Wanda and I will take the kids back to your place and put them to bed."

The strained smile on Hunter's face told RaeLynn that while he was grateful for the help, he also hated not being able to do it himself. It was good that he accepted their offer, though. Growing up, how many times had RaeLynn been left to put the kids to bed? It wasn't that she blamed her mother for it. Her mom worked hard to keep food on the table and a roof over their heads. But seeing the family come together like this made her realize how things could be.

As they walked toward the barn, the wind picked up slightly under the setting sun. She shivered a bit, and Hunter noticed almost immediately.

"I should've reminded you that it gets cold once the sun goes down."

He shrugged out of the warm flannel he'd put on when they'd gone outside to get dessert. At the time, she'd thought it was overkill, because it had been such a nice evening. But now, she saw the wisdom in his actions.

"Here. Put this on."

She hesitated as she took it. "But won't you be cold?"

He shrugged. "Better me than the lady. And I'll be walking with the horse and moving around, which will keep me warmer. You, on the other hand, will get colder just sitting around watching. I'll be fine."

As she put on the flannel, his warm scent enveloped her. Having Hunter's shirt on her was like a giant, warm hug from the man. So comforting. It was the closest she'd probably ever come to being in his arms, and she felt a twinge of regret at the thought. He was a good man, and were the situation different, she would have liked to get closer to him.

Chapter Five

⌒

Working with the vet took longer than Hunter had anticipated, but colic often took more time than you thought it would, and nothing with animals could ever be truly predictable. Eventually, they appeared to be through the worst of it. RaeLynn looked to be almost dead on her feet. "I'm almost done," he said.

She gave him a tired smile, and even looking utterly exhausted, she was still beautiful.

"I wish you'd gone back to your cabin

earlier," he said. "I feel bad making you sit through this."

"It was interesting. I'm glad you included me."

She didn't look glad, but he wasn't going to argue.

He finished cleaning up and gave some final instructions to his ranch hand. The hand already knew what to do, so it was mostly just a reminder, along with encouragement to contact him if the horse suddenly got worse. Judging by the amount of manure that had already come out, Hunter thought they were out of the woods, but you could never be too sure. He was just glad the vet thought the horse was going to be okay.

When he was finished, he held an arm out to RaeLynn. "Let's get you back to your cabin."

As they walked along the road from the barn to where the cabins were, the fresh air and moonlight brought a greater strength and energy to him. The fatigue he felt in his bones lightened, and when he glanced over at RaeLynn, he could see that she was feeling it, too.

She held his flannel wrapped tightly against her, and he was glad he'd thought to grab it when they'd gone outside after dinner. Working with the horse, he hadn't been cold at all. He could tell RaeLynn was less used to the cold and had needed it far more than he did. Even still, she shivered slightly when the breeze picked up.

"It's not far. I should have had someone bring you back to your cabin earlier. I'm sorry."

RaeLynn shook her head. "You've already apologized for that. If I'd wanted to go back, I would have gone back by myself. I wanted to stay. Don't blame yourself for something that was my choice."

He wanted to hold her tight to him, to put his arm around her the way he did with Lynzee when she was chilly. But he was already worried about getting too close to her. Why did this have to be so complicated? They walked farther along the road to where it branched off toward the cabins. It was a far enough walk that they probably should've taken one of the ATVs, but since his was at the house already, it would've left them short at the barn.

"Sorry about the long walk. I didn't think about taking one of the ATVs until now," he said.

"Stop apologizing," she said. "I like the walk, and if I hadn't felt up to it, I would have said so. You don't have to anticipate everyone's needs and take care of them. People can tell you if they need something."

"But you're our guest, and I'm supposed to take care of you. I feel like I haven't done a very good job of it."

She gave him a small smile. "I don't think you take care of all of your guests as well as you're taking care of me."

He smiled back. "I suppose you're right. The truth is I like you, and I like having you around. And I like doing nice things for you."

The expression on her face made him wonder if he'd been too forward. If he'd said too much. He probably had. He didn't have a whole lot of experience with women. He and Felicia had been high-school sweethearts, and though they'd broken up for a little while before getting back together, getting married and starting their family, she was the only woman he'd ever dated. That was the trouble with life in a small town. There weren't a lot of women to choose from. All his friends who'd gotten married lately had found women new to the area. Sure, they had lots of women guests, but he always kept things professional.

At least until now.

Was it dumb of him to hope she'd stay? He knew the dangers of falling for someone whose heart truly wasn't here. Was it so much to ask that he'd find someone who loved both him and life on the ranch? It didn't seem fair to have feelings for someone who could never accept his life.

As they got to the clearing by Rae-Lynn's cabin, she paused. "I'd invite you in for a cup of coffee, but the last thing you need is caffeine keeping you up all night. You need sleep."

That he did, but he was also enjoying this quiet time with RaeLynn. "True, but a nice warm drink wouldn't go amiss. A cup of herbal tea would hit the spot."

She looked at him funny. "You drink tea?"

"It doesn't fit with your manly image of a cowboy?"

He tried to sound all big and tough, and it made RaeLynn laugh. He loved the sound of her laugh. It made him feel all warm inside, and he never wanted to let go of that feeling.

"I just don't know many men who would ever ask for herbal tea," she said. "But I do have some in my kitchen, and it wouldn't be any trouble to make you some."

The tone in her voice made him wonder if he was imposing. After all, she'd also had a long day and needed her sleep. "I'm sorry, I wasn't angling for anything," he said. "Now it sounds like a stupid idea."

"No," she said. "I was enjoying spending this time with you. Even though I know we both need rest, I don't want it to end. Maybe a cup of tea will help us both relax."

He followed her into the cabin, noticing that she kept it as neat as they kept it for their guests.

She made the tea, then gestured out at the porch. "Why don't we sit for a bit and drink the tea, then you can head back."

At her words, he realized he'd temporarily forgotten about the kids. They were all sleeping, and Rachel and Wanda were waiting for him to come home. He was torn because what he really wanted right now was to be with RaeLynn, sitting on her porch drinking tea. But he also felt bad that others were waiting for him to come home so they could go to bed, too. It was one of the many reasons he hadn't considered dating as a single father.

Once again, RaeLynn seemed to sense what he was thinking about. "Let's take it over to your place," she said. "That way, the others can get back home and go to bed, and you can rest assured that the kids are okay."

Was it wrong to like her even more?

Of course it was. He couldn't help himself, though. He knew this was temporary, but he didn't want it to end. They walked in silence to his cabin, where only a small light shone. When they entered, the cabin was quiet, and Wanda sat in his recliner, reading a book.

"Sorry it took so long," he said.

Wanda got up from the chair, waving him off. "I've been a ranch housekeeper for years. I know the animals don't ever follow our schedules."

Her eagle eye landed on the cups

of tea they carried. "Looks like you stopped for some refreshment."

Her words made him feel guilty for having done so. "Yes, I'm sorry. I should have just come straight here, but something warm to drink sounded good."

Wanda nodded. "It's a cold night. If you'd called ahead to let me know you were coming, I could have whipped something up for you."

"No, it's okay. You've done enough."

"Oh stop," she said. "You act like you're imposing, and you're not. Rachel helped me get everyone to bed, and they all went right to sleep. I was able to enjoy the peace and quiet for a change and get some of my book read. If you'd stayed out just a bit longer, I could have found out who the murderer is."

She glanced over at RaeLynn. "Don't let him use needing to get back to kids as an excuse. If we need him to be back by a certain time, we'll let him know.

The man works too hard, and we're here to help."

RaeLynn smiled. "I understand where he's coming from."

Wanda put her book in her bag and headed for the door. "Fine. You two just continue being stubborn. But just know that I'm even more stubborn."

After Wanda left, they looked at each other.

"What was that about?" RaeLynn asked.

Hunter shrugged. "Just her being bossy as usual. She wants to take care of us and doesn't like it when we have our own ideas about what that looks like."

"It's nice that she cares."

Hunter gestured to the couch. "You want to sit for a bit?"

Even though they'd intended to sit and talk, having her next to him on the couch seemed almost too personal, too intimate. Mostly because she looked so good curled up there, wearing his flannel, drinking a cup of tea and looking absolutely like this was where she belonged.

"Thank you for everything you've done," he said. "It means the world to me to have someone like you in my corner."

She smiled at him. "I think often about my childhood, and how different things would have turned out for all of us had we just had some extra support. My mom did her best, but she was on her own, and that made it hard. I like that these kids aren't going to have to go through that."

Her expression changed, and a faraway look filled her face. She looked wistful and maybe a little sad. He reached forward and brushed her cheek.

"I'm sorry if this brings up painful

memories. I wish there was more I could do for you."

The smile she gave him told him she wanted the same thing, but it wasn't possible. Maybe it was just wishful thinking on his part. But he held out his arm to her to give her some comfort, and she slid over and nestled up against him.

"I hope you know what an amazing woman you are," he said.

She looked up at him and smiled. "I think the same about you. I never knew a man could be so loyal and faithful and care so deeply for children, especially when they're not his own."

He brushed her cheek again, and the look in her eyes brought a deep longing to his heart. Before he knew what he was doing, he bent and kissed her gently.

It was a sweet, tender kiss, and though it didn't last long, Hunter couldn't help thinking this was the perfect way to spend an evening and how much he wanted more.

RaeLynn pulled away first, doubt and confusion in her eyes, like he'd done the wrong thing.

"I'm sorry," he said. "I thought that we, uh…but clearly I shouldn't have done that. I apologize for overstepping."

She shook her head slowly. "No. It was nice. I wanted to kiss you. But I just don't know what the point is. I can't stay. I have my own life to get back to, and as much as I want to be here for you, I can't give up everything I've worked for."

The unspoken *to raise someone else's kids* hung in the air between them, and he understood. She didn't need to say it. She'd been very clear on her feelings all along. Unfortunately, his heart hadn't yet fully grasped the concept.

"I understand," he said. "If I thought it

would help, I would ask you to stay. But I made that mistake with my late wife, and I won't do it again. I want you to stay, but only if that's what you want."

She nodded slowly. "Trust me, it's as hard for me as it is for you," she said. "I'd given up on the idea of romance for myself, and now here I am with one of the truly decent men in this world, someone that I could actually see myself falling for. But our lives and our dreams are too different, and I think we have to just stay friends."

The next morning, RaeLynn slowly sipped her coffee as she tried to forget about the kiss she'd shared with Hunter.

She shouldn't have kissed him back. Not that it hadn't been a good experience for her. It had been one of the best kisses she'd ever received. Okay, fine. The best. She just hadn't expected it to impact her this way. Hunter was everything she wanted in a man. And every-thing she didn't. Kissing him had only made her confusion worse.

She'd said she never wanted a family. Said she never wanted this life. But here she was living it, and none of it was as bad as she'd imagined. She enjoyed spending time with the kids. Enjoyed the camaraderie and the friendship on the ranch. Loved how everyone helped each other. It seemed like if one person needed something, tending to that need became important to all.

That hadn't been her experience growing up. Even though she har-bored some resentment against her mother for the life they'd lived, she also knew her mother had just been doing the best she could. She hadn't had the same resources. Hadn't had people there to support her. It was too bad her mom hadn't been comfortable accepting help from Ricky. If she had,

RaeLynn's experiences as a child could have been different.

She stared out across the porch to where Hunter was loading the kids into the SUV to go to church. She supposed she should help him, but she still wasn't sure how she felt about going. It wasn't that she didn't believe in God or didn't like church. She'd been inside dozens of churches in small towns for various stories. It was just that a lot of the people she knew at church said all the nice things about being there for each other and helping each other out, but so many of them had let her down. Maybe this was one more area where she needed to learn to give people a chance. Just like she was seeing a new side of family, maybe this would give her a new view of church.

Lynzee noticed her and waved. It was too far for RaeLynn to hear what the little girl was calling out, but the giant wave was hard to miss.

She'd missed church the past Sunday, along with everyone else on the ranch, given the chaos with the children. This Sunday, it was harder to use that excuse since everyone else was going. She did have a story to write about this community, and church was a big part of that, so it was hard to justify not attending.

Tucker suddenly broke free from Hunter's grasp and ran off. She couldn't not help him. It looked like there was only one thing left to do. She was going to church.

RaeLynn reached Hunter's side just as he caught up with little Tucker. She helped Lynzee into her car seat, noting that the other two girls were already in the vehicle. The ranch SUV was nice, with plenty of room for all the children. When she was a child, she remembered how hard her mom had to save to get a van that would fit everyone.

Hunter joined her on the other side of the SUV and got Tucker strapped into his seat.

"Thanks for the help," he said. "This is the first time I've had to do it by myself, and I clearly don't have all the kinks worked out yet. Wanda is in charge of the coffee ministry today, so everyone else left early. I told them I'd be fine, but I'm glad you're here."

RaeLynn smiled at him. "It looked like you had everything under control," she said.

The smile he gave her made her feel warm inside. "It's nice of you to say that, but I was just chasing a toddler."

"That's what toddlers do. You're doing great, so don't be too hard on yourself."

"Want to ride with us?" he asked.

It would be silly of her to say no. But

it meant committing to going to church and staying the whole time.

She gave him a small smile. "Sounds good," she said.

Once they got on the road, Hunter said, "We haven't really talked about it, but it sounds like church isn't really your thing."

RaeLynn shrugged. "It's not that I don't believe in God. I just never seem to fit in with all the church people."

Hunter nodded slowly, keeping his eyes on the road. "I can understand that. You'll know a lot of the people there today. So hopefully, it'll be just like getting together with friends from the ranch."

Wanda had told her something similar when she'd expressed apprehension about going.

RaeLynn took a deep breath, trying to steady her nerves. It was ridiculous to feel this nervous about going to church.

But maybe it was because she was still keeping a big secret from them.

Columbine Springs Community Church was like every other church she'd visited over the years. She'd already driven past it dozens of times during her stay, so why did this feel different? Helping the children out of their car seats provided a welcome distraction from the aching feeling in her stomach. She had zero reason to feel nervous, but something about this visit felt like things were about to change, and she wasn't sure she wanted them to.

She carried the baby and held Phoebe's hand as Hunter walked in with Tucker and Lynzee. To anyone not from the town, they probably looked like the picture-perfect family. From the way Bella always reached for her first, Rae-Lynn kind of felt like they were. That was making it harder and harder for her to think about leaving.

The article needed to be in by the end of the week, and it was almost done. She'd been working on some other assignments, but they seemed to be slowing to a trickle. She'd called Gerald several times and only gotten his voice mail. Obviously, things were going smoothly without her. She felt a small pang in her heart at the thought of being so unnecessary. Work was what had been driving her, and she desperately needed it as an excuse for everything she was trying to avoid. Hunter led her back to the Sunday school area, where Eleanor was checking in the children.

"Oh good," Hunter said. "I know I need to get all the official stuff filled out, but having you handling the children today makes it a little easier."

RaeLynn thumbed through the notebook used to check in the children and smiled at how this tiny church still did things old-school. Some of the churches she'd visited recently had moved to computerized systems, but given the hardships the town had suffered, they likely couldn't afford it here.

After Eleanor scanned a couple of pages, she looked up at Hunter. "Everything is already in order. You're on the list for being allowed to pick up and drop off the children. You'll need to have anyone from the Double R who's helping you added, but you should wait until they pass the background checks officially before adding them."

Hunter inhaled sharply, like he wasn't expecting that answer, but the social worker laughed. "I'm sure it will all be fine. I know I've come off a little hard-nosed on the situation, but I have a new boss, and everyone is under a lot of pressure. You're doing a great job, and I'm sorry if I haven't told you that."

Hunter nodded slowly. "I know you know what's at stake for these kids. I dearly love them, and this is important to me."

"I know," she said. "And I think your love for them is going to go a long way."

Another family approached the check-in desk, so Hunter stepped away and gestured down the hall. "The nursery for the baby is down here," he said.

When they dropped the baby off, the hallway was quiet, and RaeLynn turned to him. "She's right, you know. Social services would rather the children be with a loving family. Anyone can see that you care deeply for them and would do anything for them."

The tender look he gave her touched her heart. "That means a lot coming from you. And I'm sorry that we haven't had a moment to talk about last night."

RaeLynn shook her head. "We don't need to right now. Life is busy with the kids, and church is about to start. We can talk when the time is right."

Though everything she'd said was the truth, she also knew she was stalling. She didn't want to hurt this man. Didn't want to hurt herself. She wasn't sure how to navigate a relationship with him. She couldn't give him forever, and she believed he was the kind of guy who wanted it. He deserved it.

She shouldn't have kissed him last night.

As they walked back into the main lobby, everyone greeted Hunter, and he introduced her in a way that felt like much more than just *This is the reporter doing a story on the ranch.* The eyes on her told her they suspected she meant something to him. Of course, they'd all seen her carrying the baby and helping him with the kids, which was probably something the average reporter wouldn't do. Maybe she was losing her objectivity.

Okay, fine. When it came to this story,

she hadn't had any objectivity at all. That fact became even more evident as she spied the rest of the Double R crew. Their warm smiles made her stomach hurt even more.

As Hunter guided her into a pew next to Ricky, RaeLynn just wanted to cry. At some point, he was going to bring up his regrets over the past, as he often did, and she knew she was going to break. And then what would he think of her? Would he hate her for being here all this time and not telling him who she was?

The church music started, and while she knew she was supposed to be comforted by the songs of forgiveness and hope, all they did was make her feel worse.

None of this was in her plan. She certainly didn't need to hear a full-blown sermon on the power of forgiving and letting go of the past. She didn't hold anything against Ricky, not now that she'd gotten to know him. Her mother was another story. Part of her wished her mother could hear the sermon. Would RaeLynn feel better if her mom didn't despise Ricky so much?

What was going to happen if her mother found out about all of this? That was a worry on her mind. At some point, she would know she'd written an article on the Double R. RaeLynn had told herself she would cross that bridge when she came to it, but the bridge was more rickety over troubled waters than she'd anticipated.

Ricky nudged her and handed her a handkerchief. She realized tears had started rolling down her face, so she took it. She wasn't usually an emotional person, so why now? Why this? She dabbed at her eyes, appreciating that the old man still carried old-fashioned cotton squares in his pocket.

Hunter turned to her and noticed her

tears. He put his arm around her and gave her small squeeze. Nothing inappropriate, just a small comfort from a friend, and his arm didn't linger inappropriately. But inside, her heart yearned.

She was keeping a horrible secret from all of them, a secret that had been hurting them for years. As the final bars of the last hymn quieted down, Rae-Lynn knew with a certainty that could only have come from God that she had to tell them the truth.

She'd always thought the whole church-and-God thing was like joining a club, but she knew deep in her heart that her general belief that there was a God had become something stronger. For the first time, she understood the faith that brought these people here to church, that brought the Double R family together.

She knew that no matter what happened next, God was going to help her, and everything was going to be okay.

Hunter seemed to understand her need for quiet on the way home. She didn't want to talk about what had happened in church, which was fine, because the children wouldn't have let them get a word in edgeways. They had learned a new song in Sunday school, and they were all singing at the top of their lungs.

When they got to the ranch, they drove straight to Ricky's, where everyone apparently gathered for lunch after church. She'd been dreading this, the moment of truth. She hadn't thought she would ever reveal it, but with each step onto the porch, her resolve strengthened.

Even though she usually took Bella, Hunter picked her up this time, and the sweet way he held the baby nibbled at the edges of her courage. How was Hunter going to take her news?

They got into the house, and RaeLynn found Ricky off by himself, staring out one of the windows as he sipped on a glass of ice tea. RaeLynn walked over to him.

"Thank you for your handkerchief," she said.

Ricky smiled at her tenderly, just like she'd always imagined a grandfather would.

Except he didn't know yet.

"It was a powerful sermon," Ricky said. "I don't blame you for getting a little teary-eyed. I hope it did you some good, and that you were able to give your troubles to the Lord."

RaeLynn nodded. "It did, but it also made things a little more difficult for me. You see, I have something I need to ask your forgiveness for."

Ricky stared at her. "You couldn't possibly have done anything that would make me need to forgive you. You've got a good heart. Anyone can see that. I know you'd never intentionally hurt me."

The man was laying it on thick, and her stomach was back in knots. Even though she'd never done much praying, she took a deep breath and said a quick prayer.

Feeling calmer, she said, "Ricky, I'm your granddaughter. The one you've been looking for. I'm Luanne and Cinco's daughter. I've always known who you were, and I knew you were looking for me. But my mom said some things that made me afraid of telling you, so I vowed to keep it a secret."

The older man's eyes filled with tears, and RaeLynn's heart tightened.

"I'm so sorry," she said. "Please forgive me. I never meant to cause you harm. The more I've gotten to know you, the more I think there must have been a big misunderstanding with my mother. I've come to love you all so much that I couldn't bear keeping my secret anymore."

She was crying again, and tears were openly rolling down his face, too. At any moment, someone was going to come into the room and get mad at her for hurting the poor, dear man. Her grandfather.

Why had she come to the Double R and allowed everything she'd believed in to be so shaken?

Chapter Six

"The prodigal has returned."

Hunter looked up from the picture he was helping Lynzee and Phoebe draw to see Ricky standing in the doorway beaming. Ricky moved aside to let Rae-Lynn into the room.

"I always knew I had a special connection with RaeLynn," Ricky said. "Like she was one of us. And now I know she is. This is the grandchild I've been looking for all along. Cinco and Luanne's daughter."

Hunter stared at RaeLynn, who looked sheepish rather than excited.

"How did you know?" Ty asked, getting up from his seat. As the Double R lawyer, Ty had been actively helping Ricky in his search and weeding out all the charlatans.

Ricky looked over at RaeLynn, who nodded.

"RaeLynn has known all along," he said. "She was afraid to tell us all the truth, because her mother told her I wasn't a good person. RaeLynn used the time to get to know me before revealing her identity."

Hunter stared at RaeLynn. He obviously didn't know her as well as he thought he did, not if she'd been harboring this secret from him. Maybe he couldn't read her well, but there was something in Ricky's words that made him think this wasn't the full story.

Maybe he'd been foolish to think the

kiss had meant something to her. He didn't go around kissing a lot of women, but maybe that's not how RaeLynn operated. They hadn't had a lot of discussions about romance and dating, other than clarifying that neither of them were in a place where a relationship between them was practical. She was good with the kids and easy to talk to, and he knew a little bit about her past, but maybe he didn't really know her that well at all.

He felt like he did, but with all they'd shared, he'd have thought she would have trusted him with this.

"No offense, but she's not the first to make such a claim," Ty said. "I hope you'll understand if I request a blood test to prove it."

RaeLynn looked scared, like she hadn't expected to be met with such hostility. But she hadn't been here when people had tried to worm their way into

Ricky's heart by claiming to be Cinco's child, only to be proven scam artists. And even though it hurt that she'd kept such a secret from him, from all of them, Hunter had to believe that Rae-Lynn wasn't like that. He felt certain of that, at least. That part of him wanted to get up, stand next to her, put his arm around her and tell her that everything was going to be okay. But that would reveal his feelings, and he wasn't sure she felt the same way.

Rachel, who had initially come to the ranch in search of a kidney donor, came up beside her husband and put her arm around him. "Ty, don't push away my sister with your hardness," she said.

Ty looked over at her. "You believe her?"

Rachel nodded. "I do. Like Ricky, I've always felt a strange connection to Rae-Lynn that I couldn't explain. Plus, I see the same wariness in her eyes that I had coming here."

Rachel walked over to RaeLynn and gave her a hug. "Welcome home, sister."

When RaeLynn started sobbing, Hunter believed her, too. Not that he'd really doubted her. He remembered when Rachel first came to the ranch, how people had struggled with whether or not to believe her until the blood test had come back. He could see how this might have been hard for RaeLynn as well.

It didn't make things better, but he understood.

The kids, who had been quiet up to this point in response to the seriousness of the adults, gave his warring heart a welcome respite.

"Daddy!" Lynzee shouted.

He looked over to see that Phoebe had grabbed one of the crayons and was scribbling on Lynzee's paper.

Tucker took the opportunity to grab a crayon of his own and do the same. What had started out as Lynzee's drawing of a green Jesus, because green was the prettiest color in the whole wide world, was now a mass of scribbles.

"My Jesus," Lynzee wailed.

"He's not green," Phoebe said. "He's brown. My mommy says so."

Phoebe hadn't spoken much of her mother since the arrest. She'd asked if her mom was okay, and at night when they said their bedtime prayers, they always made sure to include Sadie. Even though the kids were fighting over a drawing, Hunter had to wonder if maybe this fight was less about color and more about a little girl who missed her mom and didn't have the right words to express it.

"You probably miss her a lot," Hunter said, opening his arm to Phoebe. "Maybe you can make your own picture of Jesus, and we can send it to her."

"But mine is still ruined," Lynzee said, sounding forlorn. Hunter thought about how he could encourage the children.

He looked down at his daughter. "Maybe it's not messed up. Maybe it shows that no matter how many times the picture gets messed up, Jesus is still there. Your picture changed, but Jesus didn't."

He didn't know where that wisdom had come from, but Lynzee's face lit up, and RaeLynn made a noise, like those were the exact words she needed to hear, too. He gave his daughter a little squeeze, then looked over at RaeLynn.

Based on what she'd told him of her past, the way she interacted with everyone at the ranch and the tears she'd shed in church, he'd wondered if maybe RaeLynn was trying to find Jesus in the midst of all the scribbles. He'd hoped to talk to her about the tears in church, but it was hard to have an adult conversation with so many kids around.

However, after hearing her revelation and knowing that she was Ricky's long-lost granddaughter, he suspected that was the reason for her tears.

Hunter looked over at RaeLynn. "I know you have a cynical view of family, but none of us come from perfect families or perfect backgrounds. I hope you know that we're here for you now."

Hunter hadn't noticed everyone coming into the room, but he supposed it was inevitable after Ricky's announcement.

"That's right," William said. "I felt like I was betraying my father and his legacy by coming here and becoming involved with the Double R family, but I've learned it's an extra blessing from God to have so much love in my life."

His wife, Grace, handed him their baby. "And this extra blessing needs a diaper change."

William laughed. "There's always dirty work with every blessing," he said. "But I wouldn't do it differently for the world."

William carried the baby off into the other room, and Hunter watched everyone run up to hug RaeLynn. He tried to keep his focus on the kids, since the adults needed the freedom to welcome RaeLynn into the fold, but he couldn't help overhearing the words of love and support they gave her.

How would this change things for them?

A selfish question, he knew, considering RaeLynn was dealing with far more than he'd suspected. It was no wonder she'd struggled with the idea of family. Would having the loving support of the Double R family make a difference in her life? Would it make her more willing to accept a man like him?

It wasn't fair to ask her these questions, not with everything so new. So what was he supposed to do?

He knew he had to be patient and wait. He was fine with that. As much as he had enjoyed their kiss, and as much as he would like more of the same and to be able to hold her in his arms, he had just as much on his plate as she did. Yes, it would be nice to have someone to share the burden with, but he needed to figure out how to do it on his own. He couldn't ask her to stay simply because he needed her help. She had to want to stay because she wanted to be with him.

Did they know enough about each other? How could they tell? Everything so far had been about her helping him. That was the last thing she wanted in her life, why she'd structured her life the way she had. He had to give her space to deal with the situation on her own and not add the pressure of figuring out their relationship.

RaeLynn should've known the Double R family would respond with such open acceptance. Though they all privately expressed to her that they were disappointed she hadn't felt comfortable telling them right away, they said they understood, especially her siblings. They'd all had to struggle with the knowledge and the change in their family situation. Though RaeLynn had grown up with multiple siblings, having this connection to the ones at the Double R felt like a missing piece of her had been returned.

The only person she hadn't had a private moment with was Hunter. He'd been busy entertaining the children since they'd gotten back from church. He'd given her some encouraging smiles and nods, but the thing that stuck with her the most was his comment about Jesus always being there, even if the messiness on the outside made it look like He wasn't. The sermon today had been about the power of forgiveness, and RaeLynn knew she needed to talk to her mom.

She stole another glance at Hunter, who was on his hands and knees along with William and Alexander. Each man had a child on top of him like they were horses in a race. The sight brought a smile that she felt all the way down to her heart. For the first time, the sight of the men interacting with the children with such love wasn't a painful reminder that she hadn't had that kind of love from a father figure. It assured her that not every man was like those who'd come in and gone out of her life. Families could come together and work for the benefit of all.

She pulled out her phone and went into a small sitting room Wanda had told her she could use to go and pray if she needed a quiet place. Her mom answered right away.

"I'm so glad you called," Luanne said. Her mom went into a long-winded update on how everyone was doing. In the past, RaeLynn would have been stressed about hearing all the minor problems in everyone's lives, but she felt at peace today, realizing that her mother wasn't sharing this with her to burden her but rather to just keep her in the loop about her family.

When her mom was finished, RaeLynn said, "I have some news for you as well. I'm a little nervous because I don't know how you're going to take it, but there's something I need to share."

Her mother laughed. "Well, if you're pregnant, it's just another grandbaby to love. You can come on home, and we'll do everything we can to help you out. We'll make it work. We always do."

Suddenly, RaeLynn wondered if it was unfair that she'd resented her mother and her siblings because of how she'd always had to take care of everyone else. They were all there for each other, even though it was a struggle and felt a little dysfunctional. They all did the best they could, and even though this hadn't been the reason for RaeLynn's call, she felt a deep sense of gratitude at the realization that if she needed her family, they would be there for her, too.

"I'm not pregnant," she said. "I am at the Double R, and I told Ricky who I am."

Her mother was silent, and RaeLynn didn't know if that was a good or bad thing, but she needed her mother to understand.

"I know you felt that bad things happened here in the past, but I've gotten to know Ricky and everyone else here, and they've shown me such love and acceptance that—"

"I heard he claims to have regrets over the past," her mother said. "But he's such a smooth talker, I'm not sure I can believe him."

The bitterness in her mother's voice made RaeLynn's heart ache. "I know you said you have bad memories of the place, and I'm not trying to deny them. I don't know what happened between you guys, but I went to church today, and I learned about the power of forgiveness."

Her mother scoffed. "Church? Ha. That family only goes to church to look good for the community. They expect you to dress up every Sunday, put a smile on your face and act like nothing is wrong. I had a bruise one time from your father hitting me, and you know what his mother told me? Put concealer on it so no one will know."

RaeLynn had heard that her father had been abusive, but she hadn't realized his family had helped cover it up.

"I'm sorry to hear that," RaeLynn said. "But that was years ago, and Rosie passed away a long time ago. I don't know if Ricky was part of it or not, but if you talk to him about it and how it made you feel, I'm sure he would want to make things right."

Her mother was silent for a few moments, and once again RaeLynn wasn't sure if that was good or bad. But at least it gave her an opening to talk to her mother about church.

"And you're right. Some people do go to church for the appearance of being good. But the faith of the people here at the Double R, including Ricky, have made me realize that faith isn't about church attendance. It's about a relationship with God. About belief in who He is and His love. For the first time, I understand that while people's love can change and be inconsistent, God's never does."

Through the phone, RaeLynn could hear her mother's intake of breath. "I still pray, you know. And I suppose you're right. The good Lord has always seen fit to take care of us, even though His people have let us down."

RaeLynn could feel the pain in her mother's words, and even though her mom felt it on a deeper level, she understood. It was the same pain RaeLynn had been carrying around. It had prevented her from wanting a family, from getting too close to anyone.

"I know, Mom, and I'm sorry. I believed a lot of those things, too, but I'm learning here that while we all fail, we can always work to make things better with God's help."

"You sound a lot like the people at my new church," her mother admitted. "Yeah, you heard me. Even though I promised I'd never set foot in another church. My friend Andrea just kept bugging me, so I finally gave her church a try. I have to admit, it wasn't all that bad. I still don't fit in with all those church ladies, but at least none of them judge me for our messed-up family."

"The people from the Double R don't fit the definition of a perfect family, but they make it work." She hesitated slightly, not wanting to sound disloyal and hoping her mother would understand. "I've never seen a group of people support each other so fiercely. And the people in church and in the community accept them all."

"Maybe it was different for me back then," Luanne said. "I used to hate the way people in church looked at me when they found out I'd been married so many times and had so many children. Most of the people didn't realize I didn't give birth to all of them. They just saw a woman with a bunch of children and no man and assumed the worst."

She'd never thought of what her mother had gone through, of how she might have been treated by strangers, but her open confession about her pain made RaeLynn's heart hurt for her.

"There were some nice church ladies, though," RaeLynn said. "Remember Mrs. Bishop, and how she used to give us all those clothes?"

RaeLynn could feel her mother smile from the other end of the phone. "She was a good friend. It was a shame that her husband got a job transfer across the country. I'd have liked to stay in touch, but it was hard working so much and trying to raise a family on my own."

RaeLynn always felt the sting of resentment when her mother made a comment about doing it on her own. She hadn't done it on her own. She'd had RaeLynn. But this time, it didn't hurt so much. Her mom had felt alone, and even though she'd gotten help from RaeLynn, it wasn't the same as having the support of an adult standing beside her.

"But I know my bad experiences are not who God is. They're a reflection of the reason we need God," Luanne said.

"I'm glad to hear that," RaeLynn told her mother. "I think we're both guilty of letting bad experiences cloud our judgment in ways that make us lose our objectivity."

Her mother laughed softly. "That's something, coming from a journalist. But you're right. Even though bad memories are the first ones that pop up in my mind when I think of churches, there are also a lot of good ones. Memories of good churches, good people and the unchanging love of God."

Her words brought a warmth to RaeLynn's heart that made the healing she'd found today complete. "Funny that you say that, because the unchanging love of God seems to be a theme that I've encountered a lot today."

Her relationship with her mother had never been broken, but this conversation definitely brought a new level of healing and a closeness RaeLynn couldn't ever remember having.

"Ricky asked me to tell you that you're welcome here if you ever wanted to come to the ranch. He hopes you two can make amends, but he isn't sure if you'll be open to talking to him."

Her mother was quiet for a moment, and RaeLynn wondered if she'd pushed too hard.

But then Luanne said, "I think I'd like that. We've been talking a lot about bitterness in Bible study, and how hanging on to grudges only hurts the one holding the grudge, not the person we want punished. From what I've seen of Ricky's interviews over the years, it sounds like he's suffered a lot. Maybe it's time we put an end to all of it."

RaeLynn hadn't expected it to be so simple. Within minutes, they'd made arrangements for her mother to come. Since she was staying in a two-bedroom cabin, there would be plenty of room for Luanne there. There was no need for the ranch to make extra arrangements, but RaeLynn was sure Ricky would have if they'd needed to. When she went back out into the main room, the horse race had ended, and the doors to the large patio were open. Everyone had moved outside and was playing some kind of game.

Except for Hunter. He was stretched

out in a rocking chair on the corner of the porch, Bella asleep on his chest.

The sight took her breath away, even though she'd seen it before. It must be the way he got the baby to calm down. Wanda stepped beside her.

"There isn't a more beautiful sight in the world, is there?"

RaeLynn shook her head. "I don't think so. It shouldn't surprise me, because I know what kind of man he is, but it always warms my heart to see how much he loves that little girl."

Wanda nodded. "I always thought it was a shame that his wife died before they could grow their family. She wasn't cut out for the ranch, though. That's the trouble with men like Hunter. He is everything a woman says she wants, but when it comes right down to it, a lot of women can't handle ranch life."

Was that a warning? If so, RaeLynn didn't need it. She already knew this wasn't the life she wanted. Yes, she loved being out here, but part of her was aching to get back to work, to run the magazine and write stories that mattered.

"Those women would be foolish to not understand that his love of this place is what makes him who he is," Rae-Lynn said. "I hope he finds someone who can."

Wanda nodded slowly, like an understanding had passed between them about Hunter.

A group of kids ran past, shouting gleefully. Hunter stirred slightly, adjusted the baby on his chest and slept on.

It was tempting to want a life like this for herself. When she looked upon his handsome face, she wanted to kiss him again, like she had last night. But people didn't upend their entire lives simply because of an amazing kiss. Of course, even she wasn't foolish enough to believe that what she was feeling was just a result of that one kiss. She wouldn't have kissed him if it hadn't been for the depth of his heart.

She shouldn't even be thinking about this. Shouldn't be thinking about him. The whole situation was nonsense. Completely against everything she'd worked for. Everything she'd dreamed of. She needed to get back to her cabin and finish writing her article. She turned to tell Wanda that she was leaving, but Ricky approached.

"Everything okay?" Ricky's wrinkled face showed lines of concern, and RaeLynn wanted to hug him for it. She couldn't believe he'd responded so positively to her news. She'd thought they might be mad at her for hiding everything from them. But each of her siblings had their own story, so maybe they just understood that RaeLynn had needed to do it her way.

"Everything's fine," she said. "I just talked to my mom, and she's agreed to come for a short visit while I'm still here."

Wanda immediately started talking about making arrangements, but Rae-Lynn shook her head. "None of that is necessary. She can stay with me in my cabin. She doesn't want or need a fuss."

She looked over at Ricky. "I think the Lord has been working on her heart as well. It will be good for both of you to talk."

Ricky nodded slowly. "I can't tell you how much I regret driving my son away, making your mother feel like she couldn't come to me after his death. She sure did a good job of hiding."

RaeLynn shrugged. "That's something you two can talk about for sure.

Just don't be too hard on her. She did the best she could."

Ricky held his arms out to her and gave her a hug. "I know. It's all any of us can do."

Ricky held his arms out to her and
gave her a hug. "I know. It's all any of
us can do."

Chapter Seven

Hunter woke with a start. He hadn't intended to fall asleep, but he realized he'd taken a nap with the baby while sitting in the rocker on Ricky's porch. It had been a long time since he'd been tired like this. Felicia had suffered from postpartum depression, and he'd been the one to take care of Lynzee for the most part, but he hadn't also had to raise a toddler and two preschoolers at the same time. He was bone tired.

His phone buzzed in his pocket, and he shifted his weight slightly to pull it out without disturbing the baby. Many guys didn't like babies or understand them the way he did. He'd loved taking care of Lynzee when she was an infant, and it was nice doing it again, especially since he wasn't sure if he'd ever get the chance to in the future. Call him foolish, but he was taking advantage of every moment with this one.

A glance at caller ID told him he couldn't ignore this call. Dale, one of his ranch hands, would only call on a Sunday night if it was an emergency. He answered the phone quietly and listened to what Dale had to say. The east fence was down again, and it needed to be fixed right away.

Chris Jones, who lived on the other side of the fence, would call and complain if their cattle got out. Technically, that wasn't the Double R's problem. If Chris Jones didn't want cattle on his land, it was his responsibility to fence them out. But he was originally from the city and didn't understand that. Rather than listen to reason, he would call and complain to the sheriff, and even though the sheriff would politely tell him there was nothing he could do, it still caused problems for the ranch.

Making nice with the neighbors was one of Hunter's jobs. The cattle had gotten out there multiple times over the past couple of weeks, so Hunter needed to be there to make sure the job got done correctly. He shifted the baby in his arms and got up. Wanda spied him and rushed over.

"You go back and sit down. You need to rest. What can I get you?"

"Actually," he said, "I need someone to watch the kids for me. I just got a call that the fence is down on the east side, so I need to go figure out what's happening."

Ricky and RaeLynn joined them.

"What's this about the east fence being down?" Ricky asked. "I thought we fixed that the other day."

Hunter nodded. "That's what I thought. But I can't see him cutting our fence and then being angry about it."

Ricky nodded thoughtfully. "True," he said. "There's that fellow just south of him that I don't think has a lick of sense. Jones called me the other day to complain about our cattle being on his land. I sent some guys over there to look into it, but they told me the cattle weren't ours. I'll check in with them to see if they remember who the cattle belonged to."

Hunter nodded. The rancher in question was new to ranching. He was one of those guys who'd had a midlife crisis, quit his corporate job and decided to become a rancher without knowing anything about the business. They'd all tried to be helpful and give him advice, but it seemed like most of the time they all just dealt with headache after headache caused by this guy.

"I'll do some looking around while I'm there and see if I can figure anything out," Hunter said.

Ricky patted him on the back. "Good, good. It's always reassuring to know I can count on you."

Hunter appreciated the trust Ricky put in him, even if it sometimes complicated things. Like now. He shifted the baby in his arms and looked over at Wanda. "So will you be able to watch the kids for me?"

Wanda hesitated, and Hunter realized his mistake. Wanda had a Bible study with her lady friends on Sunday nights. He felt like an idiot for not remembering.

Before Wanda could respond, Rae-Lynn said, "I can watch them for you," she said.

The way RaeLynn looked at Wanda told him that she'd remembered about the Bible study. That only made him feel worse. And here RaeLynn was jumping in to help with the kids again when she'd made it clear this wasn't the life she wanted for herself. He'd felt bad enough when she'd helped with the kids before, but now that he knew she was Ricky's granddaughter, he felt even worse.

He looked from her to Ricky, then back at her. "Ricky just found out that you're his granddaughter. I don't want to take you away from him."

Ricky shook his head. "You know those kids are number one priority to me. The fence situation needs to be straightened out, and the kids need to be taken care of. It seems to me that if a good woman who loves the kids like RaeLynn does offers to help, you should take her up on her offer."

Of course Ricky would say that, but the older man hadn't grown as close to RaeLynn as Hunter had so he likely didn't realize what this meant to Rae-Lynn.

Since kissing her, Hunter had been thinking a lot about a relationship with her and what it would be like to love her. That had made him think a lot about his previous marriage and where he'd failed. He hadn't put his wife's needs ahead of his own. Granted, he hadn't recognized just how badly she'd needed to be off the ranch. But since he knew this wasn't the life RaeLynn wanted for herself, it seemed unfair of him to ask her to share it with him.

Part of him hoped that as she bonded with Ricky, she'd want to stay of her own accord. But he didn't want her to stay because she felt obligated to help him with the kids. He'd let her help for now, but he was going to have to find a way to wean himself off needing her so much.

Before he'd fallen asleep, he'd overheard Katie and Sam, elated at having another aunt, ask her if this meant she would stay at the ranch forever like everyone else. RaeLynn had told them she had to get back to Denver but had promised to visit often.

Yes, her siblings had said the same thing. But RaeLynn had a strong reason to leave. And he knew the foolishness in trying to make someone stay if they didn't want to be here.

It seemed that out of everyone here, she had the best bond with the kids. She loved them, and they loved her. That was the real trouble. They'd all bonded with RaeLynn. It would be better for the kids and him if he stopped relying on her so much.

As much as it pained him to do so, he needed to create distance between them. He'd accept RaeLynn's help to-night, but he'd work on finding other solutions for the future. Letting her go was going to be hard enough on his heart. He wasn't about to let the kids get hurt, too.

RaeLynn closed her laptop and looked out her window. Gerald had liked her article on the Double R so much that he'd asked her to stay in Columbine Springs and do a bigger community spotlight, sharing other stories in the community. When she'd told him she'd had to leave out many things in order to make her word count on the ranch ar-ticle, he'd decided that the larger com-munity deserved recognition.

This was a good thing because it gave her the opportunity to stay at the Dou-ble R a little longer, and it also gave her hope that perhaps he wasn't going to sell the magazine after all. He hadn't said as much, and he'd dodged her question when she'd asked him directly. She was worried that he was in negotiations and so couldn't reveal anything confidential. But if a deal was in the works, surely he wouldn't want her to spend so much time and energy on a great spotlight.

She saw Hunter's SUV pull up to his cabin. She hadn't really talked to him much during the past couple of days since watching the kids Sunday night. She'd have liked more than a quick wave hello or chatter over dinner at the ranch, especially since they hadn't talked about the kiss yet. She was still thinking about it, still wondering what it would be like to have more with him. Sometimes she indulged herself in the fantasy of staying at the ranch, pursuing what might be between her and Hunter, getting to know her family better.

Of course, that would never happen.

She'd always be able to come here for visits, like she did with the rest of her family. Like her mom was going to be doing today. But visits wouldn't be enough for a relationship with Hunter.

She smiled as the children ran from the car and into the house. Hunter was getting the hang of things, and for that she was glad. Another car pulled up, and she recognized it as belonging to the social worker.

She said a prayer that it would go well and that Hunter would find favor with the social worker. She had no doubt in her mind that the very best thing for Hunter and the kids was to be together. He loved those children, and they loved him. RaeLynn had full confidence in that.

She was grateful for the forgiveness message she'd gotten in church on Sunday. That was one of the things she'd seen beginning to heal. She was less bitter over the past, less bitter over not having a childhood so that she could take care of everyone else. Actually, she was better in general. Like a weight had come off her chest, and that despite the hardships, the good that had come out of it was worth all the pain she suffered.

The blessing of having the insight from her past was that she understood how to help Hunter. And, in helping him, she was finding healing for her heart. Her phone beeped with the text from her sister, and when she opened it, it was a picture of her niece in her new dress.

RaeLynn sent the obligatory hearts and smileys, noting that her heart didn't feel so heavy anymore as she did so. Usually, when her sister texted her, she got a sinking feeling in her stomach, worried that her sister would want something. But now she was getting used to the idea that she and her sister could just text, and it wasn't about wanting anything, and she realized that maybe people didn't always want something from her, other than a relationship. And that felt really good. Freeing.

She went inside her cabin and looked around for the tenth time, making sure everything was in order. She knew it was, but she still didn't know how it was all going to go. Her mom was coming for the weekend, partially to spend time with RaeLynn, but also to make amends with Ricky. Her mother seemed different, like forgiveness had changed her and she'd been released from the weight of the past. She stared at Hunter's cabin again, hoping everything was going well inside. Before she could give it much thought, her mom's car pulled up.

RaeLynn greeted Luanne on the porch and gave her a big hug. It was good to be in her mother's arms. It felt like old times as they began to chatter like nothing had changed, except everything had.

She'd never imagined herself in a situation where the truth would be out in the open and everyone would be good with it. She'd always felt warmth from her mother, but it was deeper now, like their relationship had reached a new level.

Before she could usher her mom in, the door to Hunter's cabin opened, and Eleanor walked out, followed by the children. Everyone was laughing and smiling, and RaeLynn smiled as Phoebe gave the social worker a hug. It was so sweet that it left a bit of an ache in RaeLynn's heart. She'd been missing the little girl. They'd have dinner together tonight, and she was sure she'd get one of those hugs herself, but she kind of wanted one now.

RaeLynn pushed the longing aside

and turned back to her mother. "We should get your stuff inside."

RaeLynn's mother looked over at Hunter's cabin. Eleanor had gotten into her car and was driving off, and the kids were still running around under Hunter's supervision. Even from a distance, she could tell he was smiling, and she was glad for him because that meant things must have gone well.

"Is that the guy you were telling me about?"

RaeLynn nodded.

"Such cute kids," her mom said. "I can see why you can't resist them."

RaeLynn smiled. "They are pretty great," she said. "I'm just frustrated because we haven't spent a lot of time together lately. At first, we were together all the time, but it seems like he's been keeping his distance the past few days."

Her mother nodded slowly. "I'm sure it's hard for him. Those kids have been through so much, and he probably doesn't want them to get attached to another person who's going to leave them again."

Luanne looked her up and down. "I brought a lot of men into your lives before I should have. I've always been a hopeless romantic, and I've always fallen hard and fast. It took me a long time to realize that just because I thought I was in love didn't mean he felt the same way, and it didn't mean he should meet my kids."

The regret in her voice made Rae-Lynn's heart ache. All this time, she'd been so focused on how hurtful it had been to lose these men from her life, but she hadn't really thought about the heartache her mother had been through. About how each of those men represented her heart being broken.

RaeLynn gave her a hug. "I never thought of it that way before. I'm sorry."

Her mom hugged her back. "You were a child. It wasn't your job to see that. Just like I got you to do a lot of things that weren't your job. I'm surprised you don't hate me."

Her voice shook a little, and RaeLynn hugged her tightly. "You're my mom. I could never hate you. Besides, I know that you were just trying to look out for us."

RaeLynn gestured over at where Hunter and the kids appeared to be playing a game of tag.

"From what I've heard about their mother, she's an alcoholic. And while that doesn't excuse her behavior, it does tell me that she's too sick to do what's best for her kids. But she was smart enough to have someone in their lives who does, and that's what's important."

"I know I made a lot of mistakes," her mom said. "I probably should have told you that sooner, but it's taken God a long time to work in my heart. I'm just grateful that I have the chance to make amends now."

Lynzee noticed them talking and started to run over.

"RaeLynn! This your mom?"

RaeLynn smiled at the little girl and came down toward her. "She sure is."

Everyone at the ranch knew her mom was coming, but it warmed RaeLynn's heart to know that even the children knew and were excited.

Luanne came with her. "That's right. I'm her mom."

After hugging RaeLynn, Lynzee automatically went over to her mother and hugged her. "We're so glad you're here," Lynzee said.

Such warmth emanated from the small child, but that was how the children on the ranch were raised. Lynzee loved with such an open heart, and maybe that was why RaeLynn found herself opening hers. It was hard to have a closed heart when everyone else around you was so loving.

As the older woman hugged Lynzee back, all the other children came running, Hunter trailing behind with Bella in his arms.

He was out of breath when he arrived. "I'm sorry about that. I hope we're not intruding."

Luanne laughed. "Not at all. I've heard so much about these little ones, so I'm glad to meet them first thing."

He looked slightly relieved at her words, but RaeLynn could see the wariness in his eyes. What had made him become so distant? She wanted to ask, but they obviously couldn't talk privately with everyone running around.

"Well, good," he said.

RaeLynn smiled at him. "How did the meeting with the social worker go?"

Hunter grinned as he glanced around

at the children. "I don't want to go into details in front of them, but I will say that it went well. I've been officially granted temporary custody. I'll still be subject to home visits and other requirements, but everyone seems to think the children are doing quite well here. Even Eleanor agrees."

RaeLynn wanted to hug him, but with the wary look on his face, she wasn't sure she dared. Instead, she said, "That's great news. It must be such a relief."

Hunter nodded, looking slightly more relaxed. "We still have some hoops to jump through to get permanent custody, but Eleanor said that as long as things continue going the way they have been, she sees no problem with that happening."

Bella fussed in his arms, and Rae-Lynn automatically reached out for her. The baby stretched her arms back, and even though Hunter let RaeLynn take her, the expression on his face told her that he wasn't pleased with the situation. The baby felt good in her arms, and it was funny how easily she and Bella cuddled up to each other again. She inhaled the sweet baby scent. What was it about the feel of a baby in your arms that just made you feel so good?

RaeLynn was a fool for thinking that she didn't want this in her life. The trouble was, she also remembered that the sweetness of the baby lasted only a few months, and then they turned into toddlers who threw themselves to the ground in kicking-and-screaming fits.

Hunter bent to console Tucker, who was upset a bug had landed on him. Her heart was full when she saw the tender way he ministered to him, giving him love and making him feel secure.

Hunter got the little boy calmed down and then looked at the women apologetically. "They got off their routine a little today, and everyone's cranky. I want to get Tucker to lie down a bit before we go to the main house for dinner, so if you'll excuse us..."

He looked at Luanne and smiled. "It was nice to meet you. I'm sure we'll see you at dinner."

RaeLynn's mother smiled. "Yes. I'm looking forward to meeting everyone."

Reluctantly, RaeLynn handed Bella back to him, pressing a soft kiss on the top of her head. Maybe tonight at dinner she'd get some more baby time.

They walked over to the car to finish getting her things when her mom said, "You really like him, don't you?"

RaeLynn shrugged. "I suppose. But we want different things out of life, and it seems foolish to pursue something when our lives are going in such different directions."

Her mom nodded slowly. "Do they have to be going in different directions?"

"I enjoy the children. But there's so much I haven't gotten to do with my life, and I don't think I'm willing to give that up right now."

Luanne dropped her bag on the living room floor. "You're talking about your childhood, aren't you? If only I had done things differently."

RaeLynn shrugged again. "You did the best you could. And I don't regret helping to keep our family together."

Her mom nodded slowly. "I know. I have a lot of regrets in my life, but the thing I don't regret is that I let myself love. Sure, I made some bad choices, but every single one of those bad love choices also brought me a blessing. I wouldn't have any of you kids if I had chosen not to love any of the men in my past. I can't regret that. So don't keep yourself from loving someone out of fear of making a mistake. Your mistakes are how you grow and how additional blessings come into your life. You just have to have a little faith."

The truth was, RaeLynn hadn't really allowed herself to fall in love before. Sure, she'd gone on a few dates here and there, but she'd never let anyone get too close. When she was younger, it had been because of her family obligations and the fact that she didn't want to be like her siblings, starting families too young and then struggling. As she'd gotten older, she hadn't wanted anything to come between her and her freedom to finally pursue her dreams. But at what cost?

RaeLynn looked at the other woman. "But taking a chance on Hunter means that if we get our hearts broken, there are also four kids who will be hurt."

Her mom flinched slightly at her words, but she nodded. "I get that. It doesn't mean that you have to rush into anything. It just means you need to give him a chance."

A chance. RaeLynn would probably be here for at least another week, maybe more. And then what? Denver wasn't so far that she couldn't come on weekends. Truth be told, she'd planned on coming at least some weekends to spend time at the ranch and get to know her family here better. It wouldn't be an ideal relationship, but what then? What if she did get to be in charge of the magazine? How could she handle balancing being at the ranch and needing to be in town for work?

So many what-ifs.

"At some point, we'd have to come to terms with the fact that my life is in Denver and his is here," RaeLynn said. "I don't know how to reconcile that. It isn't fair to put him and the kids through that."

Her mom shrugged. "You don't know what's going to happen tomorrow. I think you're selling yourself, Hunter and the chance of a future short by not even giving it a try. I've never seen you look at anyone like that before, and he looks at you the same way."

RaeLynn tried not to laugh, but in doing so, a strange sound came out. "He was avoiding looking at me the whole time," she said. "You want to know about trying to have a relationship with him? Okay. Fine. We kissed the other night. He's barely talked to me since. It's almost like he's avoiding me."

"Have you asked him to find time to talk? He's probably just as scared as you are, for all the same reasons. He knows his responsibility is to those kids, and he probably doesn't want them falling in love if you're going to leave. But you owe it to him, and yourself, to at least try. Set boundaries to keep the kids safe, but give each other a chance."

RaeLynn had to admit she'd been waiting for him to make the first move, and she hadn't tried very hard to talk to him. Maybe she'd pull him aside at dinner and see if they could talk while they had plenty of supervision for the children.

At dinner, she found herself nervous, looking for the perfect opportunity to talk to him. It seemed like everyone was busy chatting and catching up with her mom, especially Wanda, who'd known her back in the day. Hunter was occupied with the children, and it felt wrong to interrupt him.

Just when RaeLynn had given up hope, her mom turned to Hunter. "Ricky tells me the old wishing well is still around. Have you taken RaeLynn to see it yet?"

Hunter shook his head. "No. I didn't think of it."

"There's some historical significance there since it was the first well dug on the ranch," Ricky said. "You two go see it, stretch your legs and work off that meal."

If that wasn't obvious matchmaking, RaeLynn didn't know what was.

Hunter nodded. "I can do that. As long as you all don't mind watching the kids."

RaeLynn's mom held her arms out for Bella. "I've been dying for a chance to hold the baby."

Hunter grinned as he handed her the squirming infant. "She just finished her bottle and will need to be changed in a few minutes."

"I can assure you I know how to change a diaper," she said. "And I saw where you all have a little play thing set up for the babies, so we'll be just fine."

Hunter held his arm out to RaeLynn. "Shall we?"

* * *

Hunter wasn't stupid. He knew this was an obvious setup. But the truth was he felt like he owed RaeLynn some kind of explanation. They hadn't talked much the past few days, and that was his fault. He'd been avoiding her, mostly because he didn't know what to say. He liked her. That kiss had played through his mind more often than he'd like.

"No one goes down here much anymore," he said as he showed her out the back door and down a small path. "But it's a pretty little spot, and even though the well's been sealed off and hasn't had water in years, it's still a nice place to sit."

The sun was not quite setting yet, but it was low enough in the sky to cast shadows in the cooling air. He took her down the familiar path and smiled as she gasped in appreciation.

"I didn't know this tiny garden even

existed," she said. "It's a shame no one comes here, because it's lovely."

Hunter smiled. "I understand it was one of Rosie's favorite places when she was alive. She loved the roses and used to come sit here and study her Bible."

He watched as RaeLynn walked around in appreciation. It was a small, private spot that was the perfect place for talking. But how should he start the conversation?

"I guess we should talk about the other night," he said.

"The other night?"

"You know, the kiss."

RaeLynn nodded, like she'd known it was coming. Maybe she didn't know what to say, either.

"I probably shouldn't have done that," he said. "I know you're leaving, and it's not fair to either of us to start something we can't finish."

"I was thinking the same thing," she

said. "But I can't deny that we share something special, and I'm not sure what to do about that."

Her words hung heavily on his heart.

"I know," he said. "I can take a broken heart. Wouldn't be the first time. But I think about the kids, and I wonder how they will feel when you leave. It's clear they already love you. But they've all been through so much, and I'm not sure I can break their hearts again."

The look of understanding on Rae-Lynn's face made the words easier to get out. He'd been rehearsing a version of them for quite some time, and he felt a weight come off his chest now that they were out.

"I feel the same way," she said. "My mom thinks that I should give us a try, but I don't know what that would look like."

If she'd been talking to her mom about him, she had to feel something serious. Had he been wrong to keep his distance?

"Let me ask you this," he said. "Would making it work include figuring out a way for you to live on the ranch and be happy?"

"I have a career," she said. "I don't know how to pick it up and move it here."

"Fair enough. Would you be willing to try to figure out a way to do so?"

It was early in the relationship to be asking those questions, but Hunter was thinking about his heart and the kids.

"I don't know," RaeLynn said.

Maybe he was being selfish, but that wasn't a good enough answer.

"Let's just leave it at friends, then," he said. "I like you. Sometimes I think we could have something more, but I hope you understand that I have to think about the kids."

RaeLynn nodded. "I do understand.

Sometimes I wish my mom had made the same choice, but as she reminded me today, we would be missing parts of our family had she done so. I'm just not ready to change who I am."

Hunter gazed out across the landscape at the setting sun. He already knew the dangers of going down that road. He turned back to RaeLynn. "I don't want you to change who you are to be with me. You'd eventually grow to resent me, and we would both be unhappy. That's what happened with my late wife, only I was too dumb to realize it at the time. Now I understand that love is about letting the other person be free to be who they are and giving them the opportunity to live their lives to the fullest."

RaeLynn gave him a sad smile. "I appreciate that more than you'll ever know." She held her arms out to him. "Hug?"

He gave her a hug as requested, savoring her sweetness and wishing this wasn't, in essence, a goodbye hug. Yes, they'd still see each other, still talk, but they'd just agreed that anything more between them was impossible.

When he let her go, the air between them had changed. He would've liked for things to be different between them, but he also knew that this was for the best. He just wished the best thing for everyone wouldn't hurt his heart so much.

Chapter Eight

RaeLynn had just finished the rough draft of one of her articles about Columbine Springs when a knock sounded at the door.

She got up to see Hunter and the kids. Hunter looked a bit panicked.

"I hate to impose," he said.

He was always worried about imposing. He hadn't really talked to her other than the usual pleasantries over the past couple of days, so she could see why he might be nervous asking her for help now. The last time they'd spoken, he'd told her he wanted to keep their distance so the kids didn't get too attached. So having him on her doorstep with all the kids meant something was wrong.

"It's not an imposition. Come in."

She opened the door and ushered the family inside, realizing that her cabin was much smaller than his, which was saying a lot, considering his was already so compact. She'd never had all the kids in here.

"One of the trucks broke down during feeding on the other side of the ranch. Usually, I would send some of the other guys, but they've been sent on another errand out of town. It's just me, and I've got to get out there and get those guys home." He glanced at the kids. "Wanda is at a church thing with the other ladies. I think your mom even went with them. I hate to call any of them and interrupt. I saw you moving around the cabin, so I knew you were home. Is there any way you could give me a hand?"

RaeLynn had stayed home from a movie night at the church to work on her article. Writing had been a struggle over the past few days, but she'd gotten so much done tonight.

"RaeLynn, do we get to be with you?" The girls spoke almost simultaneously, looking at each other and then at her.

Hunter gave her an apologetic look, like he'd just realized it had been a bad idea to bring the kids with him to ask her. But he couldn't have left them home alone.

"I just got finished with work, so it would be no trouble. Have they already had their supper?"

Hunter shook his head. "Wanda brought over a container of soup to heat up, and I was just about to do that when I got the call."

He looked dejected and sighed. "I'd

bring them with me, but four kids and four ranch hands are not all going to fit."

She could tell he really didn't want to ask her to do this but also that he was in a bind.

RaeLynn took the baby from his arms. "It's okay. I know you're worried about taking advantage of people, but remember that everyone here loves you, and they want to help."

She gestured toward the door. "Let's head on back so we can get dinner going."

The kids ran out ahead of them while Hunter waited for her to close the door behind her.

She looked over at him. "You could've just texted or called," she said.

He nodded. "I know. I kept trying and chickening out. I know where we stand, and I don't want anyone getting too attached. But..." He trailed off and picked up his pace slightly.

"But what?" she asked, catching up to him.

"It's stupid. I don't know why I even thought it. We know nothing can work between us, and even though I know you're willing to help me as a friend, when I'm around you, I can't help wanting something more."

The kids had already reached the house and run inside. Even in these few precious moments alone, they weren't really alone. The baby wiggled in her arms like she wanted to be free to run with the others. She'd probably been cooped up most of the day and was tired of being held. It was hard to have an adult conversation with so many distractions.

"I know," she said. "I appreciate that you're trying to keep firmer boundaries, but it kind of hurts to have you keep me at such a distance. I miss the way we used to talk and joke around. I hate that you sit at the other side of the dinner table from me now, rather than near me. Surely, there's got to be a better way to manage things."

He stopped and turned to look at her. The expression on his face made her heart hurt. She felt bad for calling him out on his behavior because she didn't want to hurt him. Didn't want to hurt herself. So where was the balance between not hurting each other by spending time together, and not hurting each other by not spending time together? How had they become attached so quickly? Whatever this was, they both felt it, and while it seemed both wrong and impractical to deny it, it was wrong and impractical to admit to it.

"I'm sorry," he said. "This is new to me. I'm not used to having feelings for someone, let alone feelings that I shouldn't have."

He gestured at the door to his house, which was only a few feet away. "We should get in there before they set something on fire."

RaeLynn laughed. "Is that a possibility?"

Hunter shook his head. "Of course not. Everything has been extremely babyproofed in accordance with the guidelines of social services. Eleanor said I might have gone a little overboard with it actually, but I'm not taking any chances on losing these kids."

He walked up the steps and into the cabin. How could she not like him? There was so much good in Hunter, especially with how well and deeply he loved others.

Fortunately, the kids hadn't burned the house down. They'd actually gone straight to the coffee table in the living room where they must have been sitting before they came to get her.

"There's a coloring contest at the community center," he said. "The kids all have it in their heads they're going to win, and they've been working diligently on their entries."

RaeLynn walked over to where the kids were working. "What's the prize?"

"A new bike," Phoebe said, looking up at her with stars in her eyes. "I always wanted a bike, and Lynzee lets me ride hers sometimes, but we have to take turns. If I win the coloring contest, I would have a bike all my own, and we could ride together."

Lynzee looked up from her drawing. "And if I win, I'll give her my old bike. That way, we'll both have bikes."

RaeLynn looked over at Tucker, who was just scribbling on paper.

"And what if he wins the bike?" she asked.

The girls looked at each other like

they hadn't considered that. Then Lynzee looked back at her.

"He just scribbles. He is not going to win."

"I'm sure there will be a lot of entries. Someone else might win the bike even if your pictures are very good," Rae-Lynn said, trying to prepare the girls for the possibility they wouldn't win.

The girls looked at each other again, and then Phoebe shrugged. "We'll just keep sharing Lynzee's bike. But it sure would be nice to have a bike of my own. Don't you think?"

It would indeed, and RaeLynn thought back to when she was a little girl and how she'd long for things like a new bike. She glanced over at Hunter, whose expression told her that, win or lose, once the coloring contest was over, the kids would all have bikes of their own.

"There's a pot on the stove. You just have to heat it up," he said. "I shouldn't be gone too long, maybe a couple of hours. But there's parts of the range with no cell signal, so don't get alarmed if you don't hear from me."

"We'll be fine," she said, setting the baby down on her play mat. "I'll get dinner started. You go on."

She resisted the urge to give him a hug and a kiss as he left. They weren't in a romantic relationship, but something about being here with him and the kids and talking about arrangements felt right.

After Hunter left, RaeLynn started dinner. She was grateful it was something simple to heat up. The soup smelled delicious, much better than one of the frozen dinners she had in the freezer. Wanda would be appalled if she knew, but RaeLynn liked having the convenience of something easy on hand so she didn't have to depend on anyone else.

Maybe there was a little of Hunter inside her as well. As she started dishing up the soup, she called the kids. They all dutifully filed into the kitchen, which made her smile. It felt so much like home to her. So familiar and comfortable. She enjoyed her evening as part of a family, instead of spending it alone in her cabin. She used to think that she craved alone time, and while she did appreciate it from time to time, she had to admit that she equally appreciated times like these.

It did feel just a little bit lonely without Hunter, as if he held everyone all together. His presence had filled the tiny kitchen, and he was noticeably absent now. She got all the kids situated in their respective seats, noticing that since her last visit, Hunter had acquired a high chair that allowed the baby to sit at the table with them even though she still couldn't fully sit up on her own yet. They hadn't had a chair like this when RaeLynn had helped with her family. As much as she enjoyed holding the baby, this allowed her to help all the other children, especially since she was on her own. That's probably why Hunter needed the chair.

Lynzee patted her on the arm. "Rae-Lynn? Since Daddy is not here to say the blessing, can I?"

That was the other thing she appreciated about Hunter. He was raising the kids with a strong faith that seemed to permeate everything they did. She'd grown up saying a blessing at the table, but it had been a rote prayer that seemed mechanical and not heartfelt. Every prayer she'd had with this family came from the heart. It had made her rethink her own prayers. As her relationship with God deepened, so did the sincerity of her prayers, based on the example she'd been given here.

RaeLynn smiled. "I would love for you to say the blessing today."

The children all clasped their hands and bowed their heads.

"Dear God," Lynzee said, "thank You for this food, and thank You for Rae-Lynn coming over tonight. Please make her not stay gone so long again. Keep Daddy safe from all the mean cows. In Jesus's name, amen."

Part of RaeLynn wanted to laugh at the prayer, but part of it broke her heart. She and Hunter had agreed it was in the children's best interests for her to keep her distance, but it was clear the kids missed her. She didn't know how to address this. How could she? She didn't even know herself what was going to happen. As for the mean-cow thing...

"Why does your daddy need protection from the mean cows?" RaeLynn asked.

Lynzee looked over at her, her eyes

wide. "Daddy took us out to see the cows, but one of them was mean and chased us. Daddy said not to worry because it happens all the time, but what if the mean cow gets him when he's alone?"

RaeLynn smiled and gently patted the little girl's head. "Your daddy has spent a lot of time with cows, and I'm sure he knows how to take care of himself. As you get older, he'll teach you to do the same."

Growing up on a ranch, Lynzee would have no choice but to learn how to act around the animals, but she didn't look convinced.

"That's what he says, but a cow is a lot bigger than a person."

RaeLynn nodded. "That's why you have to learn how to deal with them."

Her answer seemed to appease Lynzee or the little girl was just too hungry to care because she dug right into her soup. Everyone must be hungry, because there was no chatter, only the sounds of children happily slurping their dinner.

Warm contentment filled RaeLynn as she looked around at this little family, and it had nothing to do with the delicious soup. She didn't want to leave them. Didn't want to leave this place. But what else was she supposed to do? What happened in a few years from now if the novelty wore off? She'd be stuck after having given up her dreams and her opportunities.

More than that, she still had an obligation to tell the stories of the people in the small towns of Colorado so that they were not forgotten. People needed to know about communities like Columbine Springs. When disaster struck in a small town, the rescue people who came from other areas only stayed during the immediate need, leaving the town to pick up the pieces for years afterward. The community here had come together after the fire to rebuild, neighbor helping neighbor, giving what they could, supporting each other long after the rescue efforts were done.

So much of Columbine Springs still bore the scars of the fire. There were buildings under construction and some burned-out shells that were reminders of what used to be there. It seemed like so much more was at stake than just RaeLynn's contentment. Was it fair of her to ignore her larger mission?

What about the kids? a tiny voice inside her asked. No, they would be fine. They had plenty of support from the Double R family. RaeLynn would still come visit. She couldn't discover her family only to leave them behind. So she would still be able to check in on the kids from time to time.

After dinner, she played with the children for a little bit before getting them all ready for bed. She noticed that the routine she and Hunter had established early on now ran like a well-oiled machine. It was amazing how easily the children had adapted, and once again, she was grateful they would get to stay with him and have a chance at stability.

The kids were asleep when Hunter got home, and he looked absolutely worn-out. She would like to sit and talk with him, maybe continue their conversation, but the last time they stayed up late talking, they ended up kissing, and that had only confused matters more. So instead, she gave him a smile and told him good-night.

Her mom was up, sitting in the easy chair, her Bible in her lap, when Rae-Lynn arrived back at her cabin.

"Did you have a good time with the kids?" she asked.

RaeLynn nodded. "I didn't realize it

would be this hard," she said. "The kids have missed me, and to tell the truth, I've missed them a lot, too. I've been trying to keep my distance so no one gets too attached, but I think it might be too late for that."

Her mom nodded. "I've seen how you all are together at the main house, when we do stuff as a family. Anyone can see that you all love each other very much. I know you have your ambitions, but are you sure that's what you really want?"

That was the question she'd been toying with off and on all night.

"A career is all I've ever wanted. You know that. Don't you remember when I was a little kid and we'd go to the rodeos, and I would interview all the cowboys?"

Her mother chuckled. "You were always asking for their stories, writing them down, making some up on your own. You always wrote for every newspaper at any school you went to. I know it's in your blood, but maybe there's a way to do that from here."

RaeLynn nodded slowly. "I thought about it. But with Gerald retiring, someone has to run the magazine. I don't think I can do that from here. At least not right away."

"I can understand that. I do wonder if you're shortchanging yourself by not even trying. The biggest mistake I made was not trying with Ricky and giving the family a chance to be part of your life."

Luanne closed the Bible and set it aside. "I feel like I did wrong by you when I didn't give you the opportunity to know him sooner. He is not a perfect man, and he certainly had his flaws back then. At the time, I was so worried about all the fights he'd had with Cinco, the way they'd yell at each other, and all the stories he would tell about what a hard man his father was. Cinco used to blame his drinking on how he was raised, and maybe that was true, but I think it also was just an excuse."

This was the most RaeLynn's mother had ever talked about her father, at least in a fair way. She sat next to her, hoping she would share more.

"The thing is I never really got to know Ricky. I knew what kind of man Cinco was. And as much as I hate to admit it, I assumed that he was just like his family. Cinco was always arguing with them and storming off, so when I did come here, it usually didn't last very long." She sighed. "Ricky actually remembered the day Rosie told me to cover up the bruise on my face. He says they didn't realize it was because Cinco had hit me. He had told his parents there'd been an accident with some tack in the barn."

A sad look crossed her face. "Ricky

felt guilty for not asking me himself, and the truth is I never stood up for myself because I didn't think I deserved it. So many problems because we didn't communicate."

From the way her mom looked at her, RaeLynn knew she was trying to encourage her to communicate with Hunter. But they had done that and come to the conclusion it was better to not start something they couldn't finish.

"I was a coward," she continued. "My family had their own stories of Ricky's cruelty as a rancher, and how he put so many of the smaller ranches out of business. But I never found out the truth for myself. That's something I admire about you and have learned from your example. Being a reporter, you have a dedication to the truth."

The compliment filled RaeLynn's heart, but she wanted to hear more stories from her mom. She never usually talked about the past.

RaeLynn nodded slowly. "I remember a lot of the stories, but this is the first you've ever really opened up about my father and Ricky."

"Your father was not a good man. I was young and in love, and, as much as I hate to admit it, I was foolish."

The pain in her mother's eyes made RaeLynn realize how she'd suffered. Until this trip, she'd never seen her mom as a woman. She'd always expected her to rise above as a mom.

"I can't believe I didn't recognize how painful that must have been for you," RaeLynn said. "I just hated not having a dad."

"I'm sorry for that," her mother said. "At first, I thought that Bart and I were going to last. I just always figured that he would be your dad. And then that changed. Cinco wasn't a man to be proud of having as a father. Sure, in the rodeo world he was a famous bull rider, but it wasn't until I was out of the relationship that I realized what a terrible person he was."

RaeLynn leaned over and took her mother's hand. "It's okay. I understand. It's been good to hear Ricky's stories about him and learn other things about him as well. I feel I have a more balanced view of things."

Her mother nodded. "I do, too. I hate how bitter I was against the Double R when you were growing up. The truth is more complicated than that, only I couldn't see it. My family is gone now, so I can't ever make amends with them." A tender expression crossed her face. "Ricky bought their old ranch. While it's technically part of the Double R, Ricky says he's kept the deed separate, hoping one day to give it to me and you as an apology."

RaeLynn hadn't known that, but it sounded like something Ricky would do.

"Apology for what?"

Luanne shrugged. "Even though I know that his estrangement from Cinco was just as much Cinco's fault as his, he feels guilty that he didn't do more to protect the relationship, to make sure I knew it was safe for me to come to him." She looked over at RaeLynn. "Even though my family losing the ranch wasn't Ricky's fault, he always felt guilty about the situation. He tried to help my father, but my father was too stubborn, and he could never get past feeling cheated over the water situation."

"The lake and the flood? But that was when you were a baby."

Her mother nodded. "Yes, but it took years to fully understand the impact. Even though the other ranchers thought it was unfair, Ricky owns the water rights. That's something I didn't know back then. My parents always just thought it was selfish that Ricky wouldn't share, but I get it now."

She looked across the room thoughtfully. "Now that it's been a few years and I see the way the ranch works, I think the lake and the way Ricky controls the water is probably a very good thing for the community. It just took time for people to adjust to the new water usage and distribution."

Her mother picked up one of the guidebooks for the ranch. "I've read about the history of the ranch from Ricky's perspective, and I can see where he made both good and bad decisions, but his intentions were always good. He always had the best interests of the community in mind. I've met a lot of greedy people in my life, a lot of selfish ones, and Ricky isn't one of them. To tell the truth, Cinco was, which is why I assumed that Ricky was like him. Combine that with the tales my father told of the Double R's greed, and I never gave Ricky a fair chance."

At least now RaeLynn didn't have to feel so guilty believing Ricky's stories and thinking that he had a good heart. She'd never understood the disparity between the different stories, but now it made sense.

"Anyway," her mom said, setting the brochure down, "Ricky has asked me to stay. My family's ranch is mine regardless of what I decide. While it hasn't been run as a ranch in years, he's always kept the buildings maintained. I was thinking it would be a good place for me to have a fresh start. Maybe the rest of the family will come along, too. I haven't talked to them yet." She smiled at RaeLynn, and the expression on her face held more peace than RaeLynn had seen in a long time.

"Ricky's been looking for someone to be the ranch office manager. I've done just about everything. I could manage the office. So I'll have a place to stay, a job and nothing keeping me in the city. I've missed this life, so I've decided to stay. I hope you'll consider doing the same."

RaeLynn hadn't expected all that from her mom. Sure, she was pleased at the reconciliation, but this seemed to be a total change for her.

"And here I thought you'd given up the whole cowboy world forever," Rae-Lynn said.

Her mother laughed. "For a long time, I thought that running after cowboys was the source of my problems, but I've learned that my poor taste in men was about the insecurities and wounds I needed to heal inside myself. And that's something I've been doing with the Lord's help." She smiled. "Surely you've noticed that I haven't had a boyfriend in about ten years. That's been intentional on my part. I needed to work on me and be the woman God needed me to be without looking for some man to do it for me. I've always admired that you have such a good sense of who you are, only you've done such a good job of being independent that you keep telling yourself you don't need any man."

RaeLynn sighed. She wasn't wrong. But what should she do? Just give up on her plans so she could have a man?

Before she could think of a response, her mom continued. "You're pushing away the first one I've ever seen make you happy. Don't give up on Hunter because of my mistakes."

RaeLynn hadn't thought of it that way, but she could see where watching her mother's own failed romances had definitely influenced her own. Of course, it was more complicated than that.

"I understand that," RaeLynn said. "But can you see that I'm just not ready to give up the life I've built to raise another family?"

Her mother nodded. "If helping Hunter with these kids and his daughter feels like an obligation rather than a joy, then you shouldn't do it. Having a family is a blessing, and if that's not how you see it, then you're right not to take it on."

She pulled out her phone, turned it on and showed RaeLynn her screen saver, which was a photo of their ragtag bunch.

"Did you never find it odd that when whatever man I was with left, the kids he'd brought with him to the relationship usually stayed? I didn't have to keep those kids. I chose to because I loved them and I cared about them. It wasn't an easy life, but I chose it out of love for the kids."

Now that RaeLynn thought about it, she could see how it had been a choice. She used to see it as a sacrifice, but her mom had seen it as an act of love.

Her mom gave her a stern look. "If you aren't choosing to be with Hunter and help him with the kids out of love, then don't do it. He deserves better than that, and you will eventually end up resenting them all."

"And what if I feel torn?" RaeLynn asked. "What if I do love them and want to be with them, but I don't know if it's enough to sustain me?"

Her mom shrugged. "Like I said, I don't see why you can't have both. Maybe what you really need to do is to explore how you can make it work. The future of the magazine has not been determined yet. It's possible you could run it remotely. Explore the idea. See where it leads you. Stop hiding from love just because you don't know how to make it work. Try to make it work."

RaeLynn hadn't given it a try. All she'd done was make a lot of excuses and justify why they couldn't be together. Maybe it was time to see if they could make it work?

Chapter Nine

As Hunter got the kids ready in the morning to go to the ranch house, they seemed happier than they'd been in a while. Not that they'd ever been unhappy, but there was just a different lightness to them as they went about their morning routine.

Lynzee handed him a picture. "Do you think we could go by RaeLynn's on our way out so I can give this to her?"

It was a simple picture, but Hunter didn't need to look at it very closely to see the meaning behind it. A man, a woman, three children and a baby. It was all of them together.

"That's a nice picture," he said.

Lynzee beamed widely. "Maybe it will help her remember to not stay away so much."

The knife in his heart was keener than any pain he could remember. He'd tried so hard to keep this from happening. He shouldn't have asked her to watch the kids last night, but there hadn't been any other option. It had reawakened the kids' desire to see RaeLynn, and now everyone would suffer.

The worst part was when he'd come home last night, his own heart had been conflicted. He would've liked to ask her to stay, to sit and talk like they used to. It wasn't like they could avoid each other. Now that they knew she was Ricky's granddaughter, she was at the ranch house an awful lot.

As he stared at the picture, trying to figure out what to do, a knock sounded.

When he went to answer it, Janie stepped in. "I'm glad I caught you before you left," she said. "Instead of hanging out at the ranch house today, we got an invite to go over to The Three Sisters Ranch to see their new baby goats. Sam and Katie have been dying to play with their friend, Ryan, and it'll be a good chance for all our kids to socialize with theirs."

The Three Sisters Ranch was a neighboring place that had been taken over a few years ago by three sisters. They'd been completely inexperienced at first and had become good friends with the Double R family while trying to learn. The families were connected by the bonds of friendship.

"They don't mind having an extra bunch of kids?" he asked.

Janie laughed. "Surely you know better than to ask that by now." Her laugh made him feel a little foolish, but the smile in her eyes told him he shouldn't take her too seriously.

"Ryan has been begging for Sam to come over, and we all want to see the baby goats, so this is perfect."

The picture in his hands felt especially heavy. This would give him a chance to talk to RaeLynn.

"All right, then, sounds like a plan," he said.

Janie gathered the kids, and they went outside to where a ranch van was parked. They'd used it a couple of times when going on group outings with all the children. After they got the kids all secured, Janie drove off, leaving Hunter to stare at the picture he'd promised to give RaeLynn.

He walked over to her cabin. RaeLynn and her mom were sitting at the table, drinking coffee and eating some muffins.

"You should join us," her mom offered. Hunter glanced at the paper in his hands, then at RaeLynn. "I'm afraid I can't stay. But I wanted to give RaeLynn a picture that Lynzee drew her."

He'd hoped to talk to her alone, but he wasn't sure how to orchestrate that without making Luanne think there was more to the situation. He'd noticed the way she, along with Wanda and the others, were always trying to push him and RaeLynn together. It was a nice sentiment, but they'd seemed to forget that hearts were at stake.

"No, sit. I insist. You and RaeLynn have barely had a chance to talk lately, and I'm about to head out anyway. I want to go tell Ricky the good news."

Hunter turned his gaze to her. "What good news?"

Luanne grinned, suddenly looking a lot like RaeLynn. "Ricky bought and kept my family's old ranch, and he's giving it to me. He also offered me a job as the office manager for the guest ranch, and I've decided to accept. I've missed this life. I needed to get away from it to realize how much it meant to me. I was so caught up in my pain over everything that happened with Cinco that I forgot all the things I loved about being here."

Hunter knew the old Anderson ranch well. He'd often go over to take care of things there. It was a bit far from the main Double R buildings, but Hunter had thought it could be used for private parties or storing Double R equipment. Ricky had always staunchly refused, though, saying he wanted to preserve its legacy. Now Hunter understood why.

"That's great," he said. "I think we've done a pretty good job of keeping things up, but if there's anything you see that needs to be done, please let me know."

He looked over at RaeLynn. "What

does this mean for you?" he asked. He wanted to say this was another reason for her to stay. Of course, he'd love it if she stayed because she wanted to be with him and the kids, but if she came to visit her mom often, it might be good for him as well.

No, that was probably a silly thought. He couldn't hang in limbo, hoping that she would eventually come around. It was ironic that he was here to reinforce the idea of keeping their distance, and now he was suddenly wondering whether there was the possibility of something more.

"It gives me more reason to spend time in Columbine Springs," RaeLynn said. Then she looked over at her mom, an unreadable expression on her face. "I still need to figure out how I'm going to make everything work, but I'll admit that the closer I get to leaving, the less I want to."

Her mother gave a slight nod, and while Hunter wondered what that was about, the bigger question in his mind and his heart was if he was possibly responsible for her feeling that way.

"I need to get going," Luanne said. "I'll see you all at dinner."

RaeLynn gestured to one of the kitchen chairs. "Please sit, Hunter. Even if it's just for a moment."

While he needed to get to work, he was too curious about what RaeLynn's plans were.

As he sat, she got up and poured him a cup of coffee. "Here. You're always so rushed in the morning, you probably haven't had a chance to just sit and enjoy your coffee for a while."

When she sat back down, she looked nervous, so he smiled at her. He handed her the picture Lynzee had drawn her. "I actually came by to drop this off for you," he said.

RaeLynn looked at the picture and smiled. "I'm sorry if it made things uncomfortable for you."

Hunter shook his head. "So what do we do?"

"I don't know," she said. "Part of me says that there's obviously something here, and it's foolish not to give it a chance. But the other part of me looks at what I would be giving up, and I don't ever want to resent anyone for it. So I don't know where that leaves us. My mom thinks I should give us a try."

She sounded so uncertain, and he didn't want to push her. Her fear of regret was the exact reason why he didn't want to make her stay. He'd already done that once, and he still couldn't let go of the guilt.

"You know I'll support you whatever you do," he said. "I'm not going to force you to make a decision you will regret later. This has to be your decision."

"What if I try, and I realize I can't do it? What if I miss my old life too much, and I choose to go back? I think about all the hearts that will be broken."

The fear in her voice made him want to take her into his arms and tell her it was going to be okay.

"What if you stay, and despite our best efforts, we can't make it work? I mean, there are no guarantees. That's the risk in all relationships. And it's up to you to decide whether or not you're willing to take it."

As he spoke, he realized that fear of the unknown had been holding him back. And if he was going to have something last with her, or anyone else, he had to be willing to take that risk.

"I'm willing to take that chance with you," he said. "Yes, there is a lot at stake. But I have to believe that because we both understand how high the stakes are, we'll be willing to do the work for everyone's sake."

RaeLynn nodded slowly. "You're right. And I think that's kind of what my mom was trying to tell me last night when we were talking about it. I've seen all the ways relationships can go wrong, and how kids get caught in the middle. It's made me afraid to open myself up. Never taking a risk means never getting hurt, but it also means never falling in love."

She gave him a small smile. "All right, then. I'm willing to give it a try."

Chapter Ten

Things slowly got back to normal at the Double R. Hunter started sitting next to her again at meals, and the camaraderie they'd shared had returned. Secretly, RaeLynn hoped for some alone time with him so they could maybe sneak another kiss in. But that would have to wait, because right now, Hunter was taking them on a family hike.

He had Bella in a carrier on his front, and they'd wrangled the little ones into staying on track. It wasn't a difficult hike, and it felt good to get out with the kids and stretch their legs. RaeLynn's backpack had the makings of a picnic lunch that they could enjoy at the lake.

Hunter had paused to point out an eagle flying, and RaeLynn smiled at how enraptured the kids were as he explained about the bird. She caught up to him and stood beside him.

"It's amazing how much you know about everything around here," she said.

"That's because he's supersmart," Lynzee piped up. "I have the smartest daddy in the whole wide world."

RaeLynn laughed, but then she noticed that Phoebe looked sad.

"What's wrong?" RaeLynn asked.

Phoebe kicked a rock. "I don't have a dad, just an uncle daddy, and I don't think that's the same."

It wasn't the same, and RaeLynn knew the pain of being a little girl without a dad. Hers had been dead, but from what RaeLynn had heard about Phoebe's dad, he might as well be. As part of the social-services investigation, they'd talked to him, and he'd signed over all parental rights. He didn't want to be a part of his daughter's life. His loss, but that didn't help the little girl hurting in front of her.

RaeLynn squatted so she was eye to eye with Phoebe. "Not everyone has a dad. At least not in the same way. And that's okay. Cinco was my dad, but he died before I was born. My mom tried to give me other dads, but that didn't work out. Lynzee has a dad, but not a mom. Our families all look different, and that's okay. The important thing is that you have lots of people around who love you."

She wanted to say more, but there was only so much a preschooler could understand. Hopefully, Phoebe would feel just how much she was loved.

She pulled the little girl into her arms.

"No matter what happens, I'll always be your family."

Phoebe hugged her tightly, and it felt so good, until Tucker came over and jabbed her with a stick.

"Tucker! We don't poke people with sticks."

Tucker glared at her, obviously feeling left out. She held out an arm to him, and he came over and she gave them both a tight squeeze.

Lynzee put her hands on her hips. "What about me?"

RaeLynn loosened her hold on the other two and stretched out her other arm for Lynzee to join them. "Well, come on. There is enough room for you, too. And yes, I will also always be your family."

She hugged the three children, well aware of Hunter's gaze on her. What she wanted to say but couldn't in front of the children, was that even if things didn't work out between them, she wasn't going to renege on her commitment to the kids.

She gave them one final squeeze and stood. "Okay. We still have some hiking to do, and I'm getting hungry. We're almost at the lake, so let's get moving."

The three children ran ahead, and Hunter hung back with her. "Thank you for that," he said. "She's been acting weird lately about the whole daddy thing. I think having it in her face all the time that there's a difference between an uncle and a daddy has been hard for her. You explained it well."

She reached out and gave him a small side hug. "I can relate to how she feels, having so many father figures who weren't my dad growing up. As long as Phoebe knows she's loved, eventually that difference isn't going to matter to her. So just keep emphasizing how much you care for her. That's all she needs."

Hunter squeezed back, and his warmth filled her heart. He was so open, so willing to work on things. Hunter was always willing to talk and compromise, and that was maybe one more area where she needed to learn to trust and grow.

Fortunately, they were on a straight part of the path, and the children hadn't gotten out of sight, but they had to move swiftly to catch up. The hugs had rejuvenated the kids, or maybe it was the promise of lunch. Just as they got to the lake, two of the ranch hands pulled up on an ATV.

"I know this is your day off, but you said to let you know immediately if something happens with that east fence again. You're out of cell-phone range, but we knew you were coming here. Sorry for interrupting."

Hunter looked sheepishly at RaeLynn, so before he could apologize, she said, "Go. I know what a nuisance this situation has been."

He'd taken Bella out of the carrier and set her on a blanket when they first arrived, so all he needed to do was take the carrier off. "I know you've worn this before, but do you need any help with adjusting it before I go?"

RaeLynn shook her head. "No. You go and take care of everything, and I'll see you later tonight."

"You want me to send someone to come help you get back?"

Poor guy must feel really bad about leaving, but she understood about work. "The trail is easy and clear. We'll be fine. Go. The sooner you leave, the sooner you can make it back."

He smiled at her in a funny way that

made her stomach jump. He was such a good man, and she looked forward to spending more time together in the evening.

Hunter climbed into one of the two empty seats on the ATV, and the men left. RaeLynn and the children continued to enjoy the picnic. All seemed to be going well, until Tucker dropped his sandwich in the dirt. The earsplitting wail made her cringe.

"It's okay, Tucker. We can get a new sandwich."

"My sammich," he wailed. He'd started speaking more since coming to Hunter's, but it was only because RaeLynn had spent so much time with him that she could understand what he said.

RaeLynn picked it up, but it was so covered in dirt that she didn't want him eating it.

"How about a bite of mine?" she asked. "It's exactly the same."

"No! Miiine," Tucker wailed again.

One did not reason with a two-year-old in the throes of a tantrum. Actually, she wasn't sure one could reason with a two-year-old.

While Tucker threw himself to the ground and wailed over his lack of sandwich, RaeLynn helped the others clean up their picnic to head back. By the time they'd finished, he'd calmed down enough to get him to walk with them, but she could tell his mood had not picked up.

The entire trip down the mountain was punctuated with Tucker throwing a fit over every minor infraction. He'd obviously not taken a very good nap today, and dealing with him while trying to carry Bella and keep the two little girls occupied was wearing thin on her nerves.

She knew this was all part and parcel of having children. But it was hard to keep the children corralled and maintain her sanity long enough to get home. About halfway down the trail, Phoebe stumbled and scraped her knee. RaeLynn stopped and got out the first aid kit, but bandaging the little girl's knee and giving her a quick snuggle didn't stop the tears. In fact, it somehow prompted another meltdown from Tucker.

RaeLynn pulled out her phone. She'd been trying to do this on her own and had thought it wouldn't be a big deal, but she was obviously outmatched by the cranky children. Unfortunately, she had no signal. Though the ranch had done a good job of trying to get as much cell coverage as they could in the area, especially areas frequented by their guests, part of the beauty of coming to the ranch was unplugging and getting away from it all.

She was more than ready to call the

cavalry and have someone come pick them up in an ATV, but it wasn't possible. She should have taken Hunter up on his offer to send someone for them, but she'd stupidly thought she could handle it herself. Eventually, she'd look back on this and laugh, but not today. As she repacked her backpack and tried to get Bella back in the baby carrier, the baby also started to wail.

RaeLynn closed her eyes and said a quick prayer. *Please, God, get us through this.*

She gave Bella a couple of soothing pats, bouncing her as best she could in the carrier in a way that usually helped get her to sleep. She'd just changed the baby before leaving the lake, and she'd had a full bottle, so Bella was probably just picking up on everybody else's cranky energy.

They continued down the trail with Bella screaming in the carrier, and Rae-

Lynn holding hands with the two upset children. Lynzee looked a bit put out, but at least she hadn't complained or started crying. Maybe the little girl understood that RaeLynn was truly at the end of her rope.

When they finally got to the trailhead, RaeLynn almost wept with relief. Just a few minutes more, and they'd be back at Hunter's cabin. Bella used that exact moment to spit up all over RaeLynn. At least she hadn't done it earlier. Rae-Lynn could live with a massive amount of baby spit-up all over her for a few minutes longer.

Knowing she was within cell range now, she pulled out her phone and saw two missed calls from her boss, Gerald. As much as she'd like to return them immediately to find out what was going on, work would have to wait.

She quickly dialed her mom and explained what was going on. Her mom promised to meet her at Hunter's with a change of clothes.

By the time she changed and got everyone settled, it was well past seven o'clock. There'd been no word from Hunter. She pulled out her phone to call him to see what was going on, but it went straight to voice mail. That was when she remembered about the missed calls from Gerald. He hadn't left a message, so she dialed his number and got voice mail. She left a message, apologizing for not getting back to him sooner, saying she hoped it was nothing urgent regarding the sale.

The kids were all exhausted from their outing, so after a quick supper, she put everyone to bed early with no complaints. If they woke up too early in the morning for Hunter, he could deal with it. She'd forgotten how difficult it was raising children. Then again, she'd never had four little ones at the same time like this. She was so exhausted that she wasn't sure how parents did it every single day.

She pulled out her phone and tried calling Hunter again. It went directly to voice mail again. She didn't want to unload about how bad the day had gone after he left, so instead she asked him for an update. She knew this was life on the ranch. Things took longer than expected, just like that night with the colicky horse. She turned on the TV to take her mind off things but quickly fell asleep.

Sometime in the middle of the night, Bella woke needing a bottle. RaeLynn took care of that while half asleep. When she woke again, it was morning, and the stillness in the house told her that the children were still asleep. Yesterday must've been just as exhausting for the kids as it had been for her. She stretched and then glanced at her phone. Nothing from Hunter. Part of her was upset that he'd been so inconsiderate as to leave her with the kids all night without word. This was just like all the times she'd tried to help her siblings with something small, only for it to turn into some extended thing. While logically she knew that Hunter wasn't like that, it still hurt.

She scrolled through her phone contacts, wondering who to ask for an update. She hated to bother Ricky, but anyone else she called would probably just call him, so she went ahead and tapped his number.

"Have you seen Hunter?" she asked. "When we were on our hike yesterday, a ranch hand came to get him, saying there was a problem with the east fence. He's been gone all night without word. I'm here with the kids, and I'm a little concerned that he hasn't called to check in."

"That's strange," Ricky said. "It shouldn't have taken them long at all. Let me see what I can find out."

RaeLynn felt a little better when Ricky's concern confirmed her belief that this wasn't typical behavior from Hunter.

Her phone rang, and she was happy to see it was her publisher calling her back. At least they could finally talk.

"RaeLynn," he said. "I've been trying to reach you."

She'd been trying to reach him, too, but she wasn't going to say so. "What's going on?" she asked.

"I want to discuss the sale of the magazine with you," he said. Her heart thundered in her chest. This was what she'd been waiting to discuss.

"Great," she said. "I have a lot of ideas, and I'm eager to discuss my proposal with you."

A knock sounded at the door, and

RaeLynn hoped it was news about Hunter. "Can you hang on a moment, Gerald? Someone's here." She opened the door to the cabin and saw it was the social worker.

"Hi," RaeLynn said. "Hunter had a ranch emergency, and I'm here with the kids while he takes care of it. Can I let him know you stopped by?"

RaeLynn hoped they didn't have an appointment that he was blowing off.

Eleanor shook her head. "No, that's okay. Actually, I'm here for one of the surprise home visits to see how things are going. Can I come in?"

RaeLynn had gone through the background check and was on the approved list of people to stay and watch the children, so at least that wasn't going to hurt Hunter, but she also didn't know how it was going to look when she said she had absolutely no idea where he was.

And what about her? She finally had

the opportunity to talk to Gerald, but for this home visit to go well, she would have to end the call.

"Gerald, I'm so sorry, but an urgent family matter just came up. Can I give you a call back in just a little while?"

"This is important, RaeLynn."

So was making sure the kids had a good home visit. "I'm sorry. This is an urgent family matter, and it can't wait."

She hung up the phone before he could say any more and before her heart broke a little at the fact that she was endangering her career for somebody else. She knew this visit was so much more important, but it didn't make it hurt any less.

"Everything okay?" Eleanor asked.

"Yes, a work thing. I'll take care of it later."

"If I've come at a bad time..." the other woman said.

"Isn't the whole point of a surprise

home visit to come when we're not expecting you so you can see how things normally are?"

Eleanor laughed. "True. But I am surprised to find Hunter not here."

RaeLynn sighed. "You know what life on a ranch is like. Those emergencies wait for no one. Wouldn't it be nice if they could schedule them for convenient times?" She gave a small laugh, but inside, she was dying. Everything right now was happening at the most inconvenient time, and she wasn't sure how she was going to recover from it.

Bella started to cry, which meant peace was now over.

"Excuse me," RaeLynn said. "Or come with me. I don't know how this is done."

"I'll come with you, if you don't mind," Eleanor said.

RaeLynn had figured that would be the answer. After yesterday's meltdowns, she wasn't sure what mood she was going to find the kids in. She went into Hunter's room, where Bella was crying in the crib. As soon as she saw RaeLynn, she stopped and held out her arms. RaeLynn picked her up and held her close.

"Morning," she said. She carried the baby over to a dresser that Hunter had turned into a changing table. As she changed the baby's diaper, Lynzee came into the bedroom.

"Tucker is up," she said.

"Let me finish with Bella, and I'll be right there." she said.

Lynzee raced out of the room. Once RaeLynn had finished, she put Bella in her bouncy seat in the living room and went into the kids' room. When she got there, Tucker was standing in the crib ready to come out.

"Good morning," she said, picking the little boy up.

He, too, needed a diaper change, so she quickly dealt with that while the two little girls followed her.

"Where's my daddy?" Lynzee asked.

RaeLynn gave her smile. "His emergency took a little longer than expected, but you'll see him soon."

She hoped she wasn't lying to the child, but she didn't know what else to say. She was trying to remain calm in front of the children and also in front of Eleanor.

RaeLynn got Tucker changed, hating the weight of the social worker's stare on her. She knew Eleanor was just doing her job, but she was nervous she'd make a mistake that would ruin everything for Hunter and the kids.

Lynzee asked what was for breakfast. While RaeLynn was perfectly capable of getting the kids breakfast, Wanda had always brought them something when she'd been here before with

Hunter. Now it was up to her to figure it out, and she didn't know this part of their family's routine.

"What do you usually have for breakfast?"

"Whatever Daddy makes us," Lynzee said.

"Cereal," Phoebe said, whining.

Cereal would actually be easiest. Rae-Lynn went to the cupboard to see what kind of cereal they had, and she was pleased to see that Hunter had quite a wide variety.

"That sounds like a great idea," Rae-Lynn said. "What kind do you guys want?"

She rattled off the different choices, and while the kids were deciding, she prepared Bella's bottle. She held the baby in one arm and pulled out the requested cereal.

She turned to Lynzee. "Can you get out spoons for everyone?"

"Yes," Lynzee said, running over to the drawer.

"I can get the bowls," Phoebe said, going to where Hunter kept them. They were on a lower shelf, which made it easy for the children to get them. It was good to know the kids had been taught how to work together and that they knew how to help Hunter. She went to the refrigerator for some milk, and Eleanor stopped her.

"Let me help you," she said.

"Is that allowed?" RaeLynn asked. "I don't want you breaking any rules or doing anything that would hurt Hunter."

The social worker smiled. "Everybody needs a hand from time to time," she said. "And I don't mind. I'm already impressed at how well you've been doing this morning. I don't think I could do the same."

That actually did make her feel better. "That would be great, thanks," Rae-Lynn said.

Eleanor got out the milk and helped the children with the cereal while Rae-Lynn gave Bella her bottle. They got through breakfast fairly easily, and it was good to know that yesterday's mess was behind them. Everything felt normal again, except that they had Eleanor here instead of Hunter.

Once the kids had finished breakfast, RaeLynn sent them off to play and was able to sit in the living room with Eleanor to chat.

"I'm so sorry," RaeLynn said. "I didn't offer you coffee or anything to drink. Can I get you something?"

Eleanor laughed. "It's okay," she said. "I'm good. Though, you look like you could use a cup yourself."

RaeLynn hadn't even had time to think about coffee, let alone make it since she'd gotten up. No wonder Hunter looked so exhausted all the time. How many times had he skipped his morning coffee so he could get everything in order for the kids? She'd known he was doing a good job, but now she had a deeper respect for him. He worked so hard to take care of everyone and do the right thing.

After talking for a few minutes more, Eleanor started packing up her things. "I'm really impressed that Hunter has such a great support team around him," she said. "I already knew that, but seeing it in action has shown me that my trust hasn't been misplaced. I'm disappointed that I didn't get to see him or talk to him, but you're right that I know what ranch life is like. To be honest, that was one of the reasons I hesitated to let him take the kids. It's such a demanding schedule, and I wasn't sure how he was going to do it on his own.

But now I see he's not on his own, and I know they're in good hands."

RaeLynn nodded slowly. "Thank you. That will mean a lot to him. I know the surprise part is exactly the point of these visits, but I was nervous that he wasn't here when you came."

Eleanor shrugged. "But now I know how he handles emergencies when he can't be with the kids. And I see they're safe. That's exactly what we need to know."

The reassurance did make RaeLynn feel better. But it also made her feel worse in a way. After the social worker left, she went into the kitchen to make that coffee and then sank into one of the chairs. Yes, she'd done a great thing for Hunter and the kids, but at what cost to her?

She pulled out her phone and stared at it, wondering if she dared to call her publisher back. The kids were quiet now, but what happened if they had a scuffle or someone got hurt while she was on her call? But she couldn't leave Gerald hanging, either. She glanced at her phone again. She'd criticized Hunter for not wanting to impose on others. What she really needed to do was ask for help herself.

She called Wanda, who quickly agreed to come over and help with the kids. As she waited for Wanda to arrive, RaeLynn watched the kids play and smiled at their antics. She loved them, but Hunter and his work had just gotten her in trouble with Gerald. Everything she'd worked for might be ruined now.

Wanda arrived, looking a little frazzled.

"I'm sorry," she said. "I was helping Ricky get in touch with the ranch hands to see who Hunter went out with and where they went. No one's heard anything. I just hope nothing terrible has happened."

RaeLynn would feel extremely guilty if something had happened to Hunter and the ranch hands. Especially since she was worried about herself and her career while he was out there.

"I know everyone's doing all they can," RaeLynn said. "I just need to quickly take care of this work thing."

Wanda patted her arm gently. "Of course. That's what we're here for. To help each other out."

RaeLynn raced over to her cabin to log on to her computer before calling her publisher back. She wanted to have all the information on her proposal ready to go over with him in case he had any questions. But when she logged on, her heart sank. There was already an email from him. He criticized her for not being available to talk to him. Even worse was the part informing her that he'd decided to go ahead and sell the magazine. She felt sick. There was a second email introducing her to the new owners. It was obvious it was a done deal.

Would things have ended differently if she'd taken that call yesterday? What if she'd been able to talk to him earlier today? Tears rolled down her face. Everything she'd worked for was gone. She knew the big conglomerate would never keep the current format or try any of her ideas. What about all the people she'd been hoping to help?

Hunter and her mom had asked her to give this a try. She had, and everything had gone wrong. At least she figured out quickly it could never work. Now they could all go their separate ways with a minimum amount of hurt.

Yesterday, she'd been hoping for some alone time to steal a kiss. Now she was grateful they hadn't had that opportunity to get even more attached.

RaeLynn walked into her room, grabbed her bag and started packing her things.

Chapter Eleven

Hunter dragged himself into the house, feeling more bone-weary than he had in a long time. Last night, everything that could go wrong had. What was supposed to be a simple investigation into why their fence had been cut had led to them figuring out that their new neighbors were animal lovers who thought the fences were hurting the deer, so they'd been cutting them.

At least Hunter had caught them in the act and had been able to have a conversation with them. Not that it had gone well. Hunter was going to have to call their local wildlife agent and ask him to go talk some sense into the neighbors. But at least now Hunter understood what had been going on.

That had only been the beginning of the trouble, though. When he and the two ranch hands got back to their ATV to head home, it was dead. They didn't have a cell signal, so they'd started walking to where there was reception. On the way, Jerry stumbled over a rock and broke his ankle. Since Hunter knew the most first aid, he'd stayed with Jerry while Andy continued on to where he could get a cell signal and call for help. That would have been simple had Andy not gotten lost. Hunter still wasn't exactly sure how that had happened, but it had. All three of them had been out all night. He was just grateful they'd had some supplies with them, and they'd eventually gotten help and gotten Jerry to a doctor.

Wanda jumped up from the chair she was sitting in and gave him a big hug. "I was worried sick. What happened?"

Hunter explained, eliciting sympathetic murmurs from Wanda and another hug.

"I'm just glad you're okay," she said.

Hunter nodded as he looked around the room. "Where are the kids?"

Wanda smiled. "Rachel came and took them to the playground. I'm just here with Bella while she naps."

"What about RaeLynn? Where is she? I feel terrible that I left her alone with the kids on their hike. I'm glad she got you guys to come help."

The expression on Wanda's face put a sinking feeling into his stomach. "What happened?"

Wanda's expression didn't change. "She missed some kind of important work call. She took care of the kids by herself overnight, and the social worker came by for a surprise visit this morning. While the visit went well, it did cause her to miss something for work, and I think it was pretty stressful for her."

He could see how that would be upsetting for her. And probably stressful, too.

"Why didn't she call you guys sooner? You would've helped."

Wanda shrugged. "I didn't ask her. She was so stressed out about you being gone and also about this work situation. I don't know any details, but she seemed pretty upset."

Hunter took a deep breath. She'd probably been worried sick, tried to call him and not gotten an answer. He knew she'd been anxious to hear from her publisher, to find out the status of the magazine and of her stories. Surely she would understand once he explained.

He looked back at Wanda. "Would you mind staying with Bella for a little longer so I can go talk to her?"

Wanda nodded. "Of course. It must be incredibly difficult for you to try to build a relationship with her and also make sure the kids are being taken care of."

Hunter took a deep breath. "I guess it's easier for married couples because they already have a relationship. Although I remember that when my wife was alive it was still hard to balance our time once we were parents."

"Exactly," Wanda said. "I hope you know that we're not just here to support you with the kids. It's obvious to everyone who sees you and RaeLynn together that there's something special there, and we want to support you both as much as we can."

Her encouragement strengthened him. That's what he loved about this community. They all cared deeply for one another.

"I'll be back as soon as I can," he said. He walked quickly over to RaeLynn's. She answered the door right away but didn't look happy to see him.

"I'm so sorry I worried you," he said. "Thank you for taking care of the kids."

"You should have checked in," she said.

Hunter took a deep breath. "I know," he said. "But we had an emergency, and I couldn't get a cell signal."

He ran through everything that had happened. He didn't want to sound like he was making excuses, but this was the reality of his life. He knew asking anyone to share this life with him was a big ask. They did everything they could to make working on the ranch safe, but sometimes things slipped through the cracks.

"That story doesn't make me feel any better," RaeLynn said. "What if it had been a more serious emergency than just Jerry's ankle? You have children to think of. You can't just go off doing dangerous things like that."

"You're right," he said. "We do have a number of safeguards for situations like this. Usually, someone checks the board at night to make sure everyone has come in. I'm not sure why that system failed us last night. I think we were all expecting that someone would come looking for us sooner than they did. I can assure you that we will be reviewing safety protocols to find out what went wrong. I'm surprised you didn't call Ricky or somebody sooner when I didn't come home."

"Are you saying it's my fault?"

The anger in her voice told him to

tread carefully. In truth, he did feel like she should have said something sooner, and he wasn't sure why she didn't. But telling her that wasn't going to make things better.

"No," he said. "I just feel bad that you were left all alone like that and didn't have any help."

The frustration on her face was evident, and tears filled her eyes. "I did really struggle. It was a bad day, and I didn't have time to take a breath, let alone call someone to see if they knew where you were."

He'd had a couple of those nights himself, so he knew what she meant. He came toward her to give her a hug, but she stepped away.

"Don't. It just reminded me of how much I don't want this life. I blew off important work calls yesterday and today to take care of the kids. Obviously, the kids are more important, which is why I did so, but afterward, I got an email from the publisher complaining about my inattention and saying he's gone ahead with the sale. I might've been able to talk him out of it if I'd spoken to him in time."

Hunter's stomach sank. She'd wanted this so badly, and one hectic emergency had ruined it for her.

"I'm so sorry," he said. "Maybe I could fix things if I talked to him. This wasn't your fault."

Tears streamed down her face. "No. It's a done deal. The contracts were signed this morning."

"What are you going to do now?" he asked.

"I'm going back to Denver. I need to pack up my things in the office, and I need to start looking for a new job. While the new publisher says they'll try to keep most of us on, I'm not confident I still have a place there. I need to start getting in touch with my contacts to see if I can find something else."

"Why not stay here and figure that out?" he asked. "Let's work through this together."

RaeLynn shook her head. "No. What this showed me is that I was wrong to allow myself to get distracted by our relationship and the kids. I love them, don't get me wrong, but I have to follow my dreams."

Hunter's heart hurt. He wanted to argue with her, to tell her they could find a way to make it work. But all he could think about was that last argument with his late wife and how she'd told him that being here was stifling her dreams.

The next time Hunter had seen her was to identify her body. Driving after having too many drinks had killed her. Counseling had finally convinced him that it wasn't his fault she was an alcoholic, but part of him wondered if she would've needed to drink so much if she hadn't felt stifled by being with him. He couldn't do that to RaeLynn.

Hunter took a deep breath. "I care about you, RaeLynn. You know that. Your dreams are important to me. If that's how you feel, go. Pursue your dreams. I'll be here praying for you. You find what you need, and I'll cheer you on from afar."

They were the hardest words he'd ever had to say, but every word was true.

She nodded slowly, like she understood what he was trying to say. He loved her, something he hadn't been willing to admit until now. Part of loving someone meant letting them go if being with you was going to hurt them.

"Will you at least say goodbye to the kids before you leave?" he asked. "I know you'll be back to visit Ricky and your mom from time to time, but it would be nice if you let them know that yourself to reassure them."

RaeLynn nodded. "I figured I'd say goodbye to everyone tonight at dinner. I'm leaving first thing in the morning."

"Thank you," he said. There wasn't more to say, so he turned and left. When he got back to his cabin, Wanda must have seen from his expression that something was wrong.

"She's leaving," he said, his heart aching at those simple words.

Wanda looked confused, so he explained.

When he was done, Wanda said, "I've seen Ty and Ricky negotiating contracts. This was not an overnight decision. Her boss would've worked on this sale for weeks, maybe even months. RaeLynn didn't lose her job because she missed a call last night and today. I'm going to stay here with Bella, and you need to go talk to Ricky to figure something out."

Ricky was on his way to see Hunter when they ran into one another outside the main office.

"I was just coming to see you so we could talk about what happened last night," Ricky said.

"I agree we need to address that, but I think there's a bigger issue at hand."

He explained everything to Ricky, who nodded. "You're right. If the contract was signed today, they must've been working on it for quite a while. I hate to say it, but he probably kept her here to keep her out of the way while they were finalizing the deal."

By the time they got back to the ranch house, Ricky had already rattled off several contacts he had in the ranching community who could help with the situation. They couldn't save RaeLynn's job, but they could find other opportunities for her. It wouldn't save their relationship, but it would at least give RaeLynn her dreams.

"Now go get that girl," Ricky said, nudging Hunter when they were finished making a list of contacts who could hopefully help RaeLynn find another job in her field.

Hunter shook his head. "My problems with RaeLynn are bigger than just her losing her job."

RaeLynn's mom walked into the room. "What do you mean?" she asked.

He didn't want to reveal RaeLynn's secrets, nor did he want her mom to feel bad. But they all needed to understand exactly why things were not going to work out between the two of them.

"Last night, when I left her alone with the kids because of my emergency, she was reminded of what it was like growing up and missing out on so many opportunities because she had to look after her own family. She's promised herself never to have a family so nothing stands in the way of her dreams. The situation last night reminded her of that promise."

Ricky looked confused, but Luanne nodded slowly.

"I've been trying to make amends with her for that. I thought we were in a good place."

This was why he hadn't wanted to say anything. "I know. And you are. But it doesn't negate the promises she made to herself about living her life and not letting anything get in the way of her dreams."

Ricky made a noise. "Family supports you on the way to your dreams," he said. "If we had known she was by herself with the kids, we would've gone to help. I didn't even know you hadn't come home with them from the picnic."

Luanne sighed. "I knew. She called

me at the end of her hike to ask for a change of clothes because the baby had spit up all over her. I asked if she wanted me to stay and help, but she told me she'd be fine. I should have checked on her, and I didn't."

The expression on Luanne's face made him realize how difficult the situation was for them all.

"It never occurred to me to give her extra support," Luanne said. "She's always handled everything on her own. I asked too much of her as a child, and that's hurting her as an adult."

The sorrow on her face brought a pang to Hunter's heart. He knew the resentment RaeLynn held, and seeing how badly it made her mother feel gave him more sympathy for both women. They were both still trying to heal from their pasts.

"We all could've done things better in the past," Ricky said. "But we can't go back and fix them. We can just do better now. I'll go make some calls to see if anyone can help her out."

Luanne looked concerned. "I don't know if she'll accept a job if she thinks you got it for her."

Ricky scowled. "I wouldn't ask someone to give her a job if I didn't think she could do it."

Luanne shrugged. "She still won't like it." Then she turned to Hunter. "I appreciate that you're trying to give her the freedom she needs to follow her dreams. I know my daughter, and I know she loves you and the kids. I agree she needs her space right now, but please don't give up on her."

Though there was genuine love in Luanne's words, Hunter knew it was impossible to get someone to fit into a life they didn't want. Maybe RaeLynn did love them, but she didn't want this life. And he wasn't sure love was strong enough to overcome that.

He smiled at Luanne. "If God wants us to be together, He'll find a way. I'm not going to rule anything out. I'm going to trust in God's perfect plan, whatever that is."

Selfishly, he hoped that perfect plan included him. But he wasn't going to force anything on RaeLynn. If she wanted him, she had to make that choice. For now, he was going to go into the office and see if anyone in the ranching community knew of any opportunities available. He might not be by her side while she did it, but Hunter was going to make sure her dreams came true.

RaeLynn looked around the mostly empty magazine office. Her mom had told her she didn't think the publisher's decision to sell was based on RaeLynn's lack of response. That was what many people at the Double R had told her. It would have taken time to execute the sale. Gerald hadn't made any speedy decisions.

She suspected Gerald had given her the assignment at the Double R and then asked her to stay longer to write more stories in order to keep her out of the office since he knew she was against the sale.

She hadn't wanted to believe that at first. Looking around the office now, she had to admit that her family was probably right. She walked over to her tiny cubicle and set a box on her desk. The small space hadn't left room for many personal belongings. As she looked at the few family pictures she did have, she thought about how if she'd come back to her job here, she would've put a picture of the Double R family there as well.

She carefully packed the photos, hating the finality of her dreams crashing. Most magazines these days weren't hiring staff writers. They worked with freelancers, and while she wasn't opposed to a freelancing career, she knew it was a lot of work. The issue she was supposedly working on with all the ranch stories wasn't even going to press.

This afternoon, RaeLynn was going to research ranching publications to see if any of them would be a good fit. There were so many great stories, and she hated to see them go to waste. As she picked up the file with her preliminary research on the Double R, she realized none of it had been a waste. She'd found her family there at the Double R, and her relationship with her mother and with her past had undergone healing. Her determination to realize her goals had also been reinforced. If only her heart didn't hurt so much at the thought of not having Hunter and the kids in her future.

Connie, the office manager, came around the corner. "RaeLynn, you're back. I'm sorry about all this."

"Why didn't you say anything?" she asked.

Connie sighed. "I had to sign a non-disclosure agreement. They promised me a job with the new owners. I have two kids to support. What was I supposed to do?"

RaeLynn smiled at the other woman. "It's not your fault. I just wish I could've changed Gerald's mind."

Connie nodded. "I know. You were so hyped up about saving the magazine that Gerald was afraid you were going to ruin it for him. His wife wants to retire to Florida, and this was the only way to do so. He invested everything he had into the magazine, so they needed the money from the sale to retire on."

RaeLynn hadn't realized that was the situation. She wished Gerald had just been honest with her. She could see how her strong desire to save the magazine could've made him feel like he didn't have a choice about sending her out of the office.

"No hard feelings," RaeLynn said. "Everyone did what they had to do. I just hate that my dream got squashed in the middle of it."

Connie reached forward and touched her arm gently. "I don't think any of us are worried about you finding somewhere new. You're a good writer with a lot of drive and determination. You'll find your place."

They exchanged a few more goodbyes, a couple of hugs and promises to stay in touch. RaeLynn's heart didn't feel as heavy anymore, and part of her felt bad for blaming Hunter for her problems. It hadn't been his fault. She wasn't sure she could apologize, though.

Now more than ever, she needed to focus on her career, not on trying to make a relationship with him work. They had different lifestyles that weren't compatible.

Ricky had offered to let her stay on the ranch. He'd told her she could do everything online from there, and maybe she could have. But RaeLynn knew she needed space from Hunter and the kids. They all did. Their hearts needed to heal.

When she got her things back to her apartment, she smiled at the kitten waiting for her. When she'd first arrived at the ranch, Hunter had told her Rex was hers, and when she'd left, he'd insisted she take him. He'd told her that if she needed to move for her job and couldn't take the kitten with her, he would take him back, but he knew how much she loved Rex and wanted her to have him.

She picked up Rex and cuddled him. "Am I making the right choice?" she asked. The kitten meowed, which was no answer at all, but at least she wasn't alone. Her phone rang.

"Hello?"

"This is Dirk McCormick of *Western Ranch* magazine."

"Hello, Mr. McCormick. What can I do for you?"

"I heard about the sale of *Mountain Lifestyles*. I'm hoping that the gap left by it will give us room to expand. You're a talented writer, and I've been following your work for a while. I especially liked the piece you did on ATVs replacing horses on ranches and the advantages and disadvantages of that change."

RaeLynn's heart surged with warmth and pride. Gerald had told her she was taking a risk with that article, because people liked the nostalgia of the horses and wouldn't want to read anything supportive of ATVs. It was nice to hear from someone who appreciated her perspective.

"Thank you," she said. "I appreciate that."

"How would you feel about coming to work with us, taking the vision you have and your passion for small towns and ranches to help elevate the content of our magazine so we can reach new readers? I know *Mountain Lifestyles* focused mostly on Colorado. We're hoping for something that could be more suitable for a larger group of readers. Is that something you'd be interested in?"

Something she'd be interested in? That had been her vision for when she took over *Mountain Lifestyles*. As Dirk explained his offer, RaeLynn realized this was better than what she'd dreamed of. She wouldn't have to scramble to figure out how to fund everything and eventually buy Gerald out.

Dirk would be the publisher, but he wanted RaeLynn as his partner. She could focus on what she'd already started doing and not have to worry about running the magazine. She'd also work more on planning out the vision and assigning stories to other writers to help capture her vision. It was exactly what she'd wanted to do.

She closed her eyes and thanked God for giving her this opportunity. It was far better than anything she could have imagined for herself. She eagerly told Dirk she'd be happy to accept his offer, and he told her he'd email the details so she could look everything over.

"Where are you and your staff located?" she asked. "Should I be looking at relocating?"

Dirk laughed. "I'm in Montana in the

summer and Phoenix in the winter. We have offices in Denver, but to be honest, it's wasted space because we don't use it very often. Most of us telecommute, although we do get together there from time to time. So as long as you can get your work done, you can live in Timbuktu for all I care."

Her first thought was that she could go back to the ranch. She hadn't been home a full day yet, and already she missed the peace and solitude. As if to drive home the point, a siren wailed as an emergency vehicle drove past.

But she couldn't go back yet. Staying at the ranch meant staying in love with Hunter and the kids. It would mean always being torn between her family and her dreams. She couldn't do that to herself or to them.

They finalized a few more details, and when RaeLynn hung up, feelings of elation brought a smile to her face. If she'd been at the ranch, she would have run to the ranch house and told everyone so they could celebrate with her. Wanda would've probably made something special for dinner and maybe dessert. RaeLynn hadn't even had time to go to the grocery store, so she'd probably walk down the block to her favorite restaurant and eat a meal alone. Prior to going to the Double R, she would've been perfectly content with that. Now, the idea of doing it felt a bit lonely.

She picked up Rex again. "At least I have you. My house might not be filled with the laughter and chaos that I've gotten used to, but we still have each other."

The kitten dug its claws into her, and she placed him on the couch. Apparently, Rex didn't like the sound of that, either. RaeLynn knew she'd just taken the kitten from its family. She kind of felt guilty for that, even though Hunter had said he would've had to find the kitten a new home anyway.

As she unpacked her belongings, the silence in her apartment grew even more oppressive. She turned on the TV for background noise but found it to be annoying. She switched it off and left her apartment to walk to get dinner. She'd splurge on her favorite meal and even order dessert. That would give her enough leftovers to take home and eat tomorrow.

On the way to the restaurant, the sight of all the families laughing and having fun put a strange pain in her heart. Rae-Lynn hadn't even been gone a day, and she already missed Hunter and the kids. She was seated next to a family with a baby about Bella's age, and it made the pain in her heart grow worse. She told herself she would eventually adapt to this.

When she'd first gone out on her own,

she'd felt free and enjoyed the silence and freedom. But now, all it did was make her heart hurt more. When the waiter brought her food, she looked down at the plate. In addition to her usual meal blessing, she asked God to please help heal her heart. To help the time it would take to let go move quickly and easily, because while the baby at the table next to her laughed, all RaeLynn wanted to do was cry.

Though RaeLynn had been gone only a week, Hunter couldn't take it anymore and went to see her. Ricky's friend at the ranching magazine had told him that RaeLynn had taken the job and could do it from anywhere, but RaeLynn had chosen to stay in Denver. Hunter could live with that. Or at least try to.

He pulled up in front of RaeLynn's apartment complex, hating how it lacked character and warmth. It was just a big mess of people living stacked on top of each other. But he would get used to it. He had to.

He walked up to RaeLynn's door and knocked. He heard some shuffling, and the door opened.

"Hunter? What are you doing here? Is Ricky okay? The kids must be okay, because you wouldn't leave them if they weren't."

Hunter nodded as he took off his hat. "May I come in?"

RaeLynn opened the door and gestured for him to come inside. Her apartment was neat and tidy, but devoid of any of the character of the ranch buildings. It didn't feel like her in here. The kitten scampered across the floor, and he smiled. Now, that felt like home.

"Have a seat," she said. "Can I get you something to drink?"

His throat was tight, his mouth parched, and even though he knew water wasn't going to fix it, he said, "I'd love some water, please."

RaeLynn walked to the small kitchen area and returned with two glasses of water. The place was so small and cramped. But he supposed she didn't need much room for just her. Hopefully, they could find a place they could all compromise on. If she'd have him.

He took a sip of the water. As he suspected, it didn't help anything, but he took another sip just in case.

"So tell me why you're here," she invited him, sitting catty-corner to him. "You didn't answer my question about everyone being okay."

He set the water on the end table. "Sorry. Everyone is fine. Everyone, that is, but me."

The concern on her face gave him hope.

"I'm not sick or dying or anything," he said quickly. "Unless you can die of a broken heart. I miss you. I love you. And when I told you I would work with you to make a relationship work, I meant it. Which is why I'm here."

He couldn't read her expression, so he continued. He had to get it all out before she could object and break his heart further. He at least wanted to say everything he'd come to say.

"If your dream is being here, then I'll be here. I told you I want to support your dreams, and I meant it. I'll find a job here in Denver, and we'll see what we can do to make it work. Even though your mom said she was going to move back to the ranch, she promised me that if I come to Denver with the kids, she'll stay here, too, and she will always be here to help. She says she owes it to you after everything you did to help her."

RaeLynn's eyes filled with tears. "I don't understand. You're a rancher, and you hate the city. What would you do here?"

Hunter shrugged. "Anything. I'm a hard worker, and there are plenty of jobs for someone who's willing to work hard and put in some effort. Yes, I love ranching, but I love you more."

His throat felt almost like it was closing up, so he took another sip of water. It didn't do anything more to help than the first one. He'd known it wouldn't, but at least it had given him something to do as he watched the expressions play across RaeLynn's face.

"I know I said people shouldn't give up their dreams for the people they love, but I've realized that my love for you is stronger than any dream I've had. Those dreams mean nothing without you. As much as I blamed myself for my late wife's unfulfilled dreams being the cause of her death, we had many other problems in our marriage. I would never have given up ranching for her, but I will for you without question."

He watched as RaeLynn closed her eyes for a moment. Was she praying? He hoped so, and he prayed that God would give them both the guidance they needed.

When she opened her eyes, she said, "I've never asked you to give up ranching."

He nodded. "I know. But if that's what I need to do to be with you while you pursue your dreams, I'm willing to do so. And like I said, your mom has already committed to living wherever we do so that we'll have her help with the kids whenever we need it."

Tears streamed down her face, and he didn't know what that meant. He held out his hand to her, hoping they were happy tears. Healing tears. Something that meant they had a chance.

"Please tell me we can work this out together," he said.

RaeLynn took his hand as she nodded. "I've missed the ranch so much. I hate the silence in my apartment. I was so scared of losing everything I've worked for." She shook her head. "But right now, getting everything I want doesn't feel like winning, either."

He squeezed her hand. "Then, let's figure out a way to win together. I've been doing fine with the kids on my own, but it feels better with you by my side. When we're a team."

RaeLynn got up and reached for him, putting her arms around him. "Then, let's make this work. The truth is my dream is empty without the people I love beside me. I kept wanting to call you and talk to you the way we used to, to share all of these moments and accomplishments. Without you, success felt like just another check mark on my to-do list."

He held her tightly, breathing in her warmth and the smell of her citrusy shampoo. He liked that she didn't smell too girlie, and he breathed deeply, hoping there would be more of this in his future.

She pulled away, sat next to him and took his hands in hers.

"Does this mean you love me as much as I love you?" he asked.

RaeLynn nodded. "Yes. If you look in my bedroom, you'll see I have a bag already packed to go back to the ranch. I was working up the courage to do so, and now I want to pack up my whole apartment."

Her shoulders rose and fell as she took a deep breath. "Do you think my mom meant it when she said she'd come and help take care of the kids?"

He pulled his phone out of his pocket.

"You can call her if you like. Ricky said that family supports each other in chasing their dreams. Your family wants to support you. The question is will you let them?"

Tears streamed down her face again. "I didn't know what it was like to have support until I came to the Double R. Now that I know what it's like to be supported, I don't want to live without it."

He pulled her close to him. "Then, don't. Come home. Marry me. Let's be a real family."

She pulled away and looked up at him. "Did you just propose to me?"

He laughed. "Well, I didn't mean for it to come out quite that way. I've got a ring in my truck, and I was going to take you to a nice restaurant and do it properly. You know, like they do in the movies. It just felt right to do it now, to express my commitment to you. This isn't me saying I want to date you and see if we can make it work. This is me telling you I want to marry you and do whatever it takes to make it work. There's no question about if it's going to work out, just me telling you we will make it work. I'm willing to make whatever sacrifices are necessary for that to happen."

She hugged him tightly, and the tension in his throat finally relaxed. He could feel her warmth and love and strength when she looked up at him.

"I want that, too. Yes, I'll marry you." Then a twinkle came to her eye. "But you know that kiss we said was a mistake, the one we didn't want to happen again?"

He nodded.

"I want a lot more of those, including right now."

When he bent to kiss her, she met him more than halfway. This kiss was way better than their first because it was filled with hope and the promise of a commitment to a lifetime of love, support and chasing their dreams together.

Denise Fawne 355

better than their first, because it was
filled with hope and the promise of a
commitment to a lifetime of love, support and chasing their dreams together.

Epilogue

"It's today! It's today!" Phoebe's excitement brought a smile to Hunter's face. They'd had the kids for just over a year, but today was the day they got to go back to live with Sadie permanently.

During her time in jail, Sadie had gone through counseling. And, while they all would have helped her had it been the case, she was not expecting another baby. She'd also developed a relationship with Christ. Upon her release, she'd worked with social services to do everything she needed to get the kids back in her life permanently. She was sober now and had a job.

She'd been just a few credits shy of getting her beauty degree when she'd gotten pregnant with Phoebe. She'd worked in the prison hair salon and learned more hair techniques, and after her release, she'd gotten those last remaining credits to earn her cosmetology license. The salon in town had hired her, and she was one of their most devoted employees.

RaeLynn hugged Phoebe to her. "I know you're excited, but go do one last check of your room to make sure you got everything."

After they got married, Ricky had offered them a larger cabin on the property, closer to RaeLynn's mom's ranch. Though the two older girls still shared a room, they'd been able to put Tucker and Bella into their own rooms, and RaeLynn had a home office.

Hunter looked around the large family room where they spent most of their time. It was going to feel mighty empty when Sadie's three kids left. But she was their mom, and this was the whole reason he'd taken the kids in. They were family. They belonged together.

Lynzee, Phoebe and Tucker all ran into the room.

"She's here," they all shouted together. Phoebe turned to Bella, who had been sitting in the corner of the room playing with her blocks. "Come on, Bella. Mom's here."

Bella picked up a block and threw it at her. Then she got up and toddled over to her sister. While the kids raced out of the room to go to the front door, RaeLynn hung back. Hunter turned to her. "What's wrong? This is what we've been working toward."

The front door slammed, and Hunter knew it was because the kids had all run out, even though they knew it was against the rules. He couldn't blame them, though. They were all so excited to finally be reunited with their mother.

"It's already too quiet in here," Rae-Lynn said. "I know they were never ours, but I'm really going to miss them."

Hunter held her tightly against him. "I know. It's not like we're never going to see them again. Sadie has been at all the family events, and she's promised to continue doing so."

RaeLynn pulled away. "It's going to be so quiet in our house with just us and Lynzee."

He pulled her close again and kissed her. "With all the kids on this ranch, our house will never be empty."

She looked up at him, her eyes wet with tears. "I know I said I never wanted a family of my own, but am I allowed to change my mind on that? I'm going to miss having a baby in the house, and now that I know what a joy family can be and that I won't be doing it on my own, I'm wondering how you'd feel about trying for one."

His heart did a double backflip. "How I'd feel?" Hunter grinned, feeling like his smile was going to split his face. "I've been praying for the day you would ask. Ever since I saw how hard Sadie was working to get the kids back and I knew they would inevitably leave, I've been praying that God would see fit to fill our house again. If you want to have a baby, count me in."

As he pulled her into his arms, the sound of the kids laughing and yelling with Sadie filled their ears.

Maybe theirs wasn't a conventional family, but God had given them something even better.

* * * * *

*If you enjoyed this story,
be sure to pick up
the rest of the books
in Danica Favorite's
Double R Legacy miniseries:*

**The Cowboy's Sacrifice
His True Purpose
A True Cowboy**

Available now from Love Inspired!

Dear Reader,

I pray that by the time this book comes out, COVID season will be behind us, and our lives will all be in a much better place. This has been one of the most difficult seasons of my life for a variety of reasons, but to have to manage everything during a global pandemic has made it even worse. I would not have been able to write this book without the loving support of friends and family.

When I came up with the idea for this book, I never imagined I would be living my own version of needing help from others. But that is what true love and friendship is: being there for those who need you and accepting help from others.

Regardless of what season of life you're in, I pray you have loving support to carry you through. And, if you're able, that you can be that support for someone else. We all need each other, so let's do what we can to be there for one another.

I love hearing from my readers, so if you want to keep in touch, please contact me at DanicaFavorite.com.

May you and your family continue to abide in God's love.

Danica Favorite